Also by Thomas Gately Briody

Rogue's Isles
Rogue's Justice

ROGUE'S WAGER

ROGUE'S WAGER

THOMAS GATELY BRIODY

ST. MARTIN'S PRESS
New York

A THOMAS DUNNE BOOK.
An imprint of St. Martin's Press.

Library of Congress Cataloging-in-Publication Data

Briody, Thomas Gately.
    Rogue's wager : a Michael Carolina mystery / Thomas Gately Briody.
        p.   cm.
    "A Thomas Dunne book"
    ISBN 0-312-16990-6
    I. Title.
    PS3552.R4886R65   1997
    813' .54—dc21   97-19588
                                                CIP

First Edition: November 1997

10 9 8 7 6 5 4 3 2 1

*For Scott Francis Briody, a fine fellow who,
to my knowledge, only bets on sure things.*

*And of course, for Karen, Victoria, and Alexandra,
the joys of my life.*

ACKNOWLEDGMENTS

My special thanks to Hannah Thomson, Neal Bascomb, and Tom Dunne, for their warmth and guidance, as well as to Ed Novak, for his support, insight, and his friendship.

I could not have written this book without the benefit of William G. McLoughlin's *Rhode Island: A History*. Pamel Watts offered unique perspective on the *Gaspee* parade. C.T. shared very special knowledge about those who hunt quahogs under the midnight sun. Any mistakes in the text are mine and mine alone.

As always, this truly is a work of fiction. While many of the places are real, some locations have been altered slightly to suit the requirements of character, plot, and all that stuff. Any resemblance of the characters to real people, living or dead, indicted or unindicted, skinny, obese, hairless, hirsute, sane or postelectroshock, is both unintentional and entirely coincidental.

TGB
April 1997

Hail! Realm of rogues, renown'd for fraud and guile,
All hail; ye knav'ries of yon little isle.
There prowls the rascal, cloth'd with legal pow'r,
To snare the orphan, and the poor devour;
The crafty knave his creditors besets,
And advertising pays his debts;
Bankrupts their creditors with rage pursue,
No stop, no mercy from the debtor crew.
Arm'd with new tests, the licens'd villain bold,
Presents his bills, and robs them of their gold;
Their ears, though rogues and counterfeiters lose,
No legal robber fears the gallows noose.

Each weekly print new lists of cheats proclaims,
Proud to enroll their knav'ries and their names;
The wiser race, the snares of law to shun,
Like Lot from Sodom, from Rhode Island run.

–from a Connecticut newspaper, 1787

M itty Navel eased his skiff out of the slip, bent on mild destruction.

It was a few hours before dawn. The new moon made it black as tar on Narragansett Bay, and the tide was low. Mitty rowed, heaving on a pair of long, slender oars to get his skiff clear of the dock. He could feel the salt air dampen his skin, while seaweed stink filled his nostrils. Mitty couldn't wait to get his boat into open water, to fire up his engines and haul ass.

Mitty was not his given name. His mother christened him Timothy, after a great uncle who left her a five-thousand-dollar inheritance, and a donkey eaten by starving men in an ancient rock and roll song. She did not marry his father, who worked as a hot walker at the old Narragansett racetrack, back when there were still horses to be walked and races to be run. But the track had been closed twenty years, and it had been nearly that long since Timmy's old man, stone drunk, walked in front of a truck coming out of a tavern.

Timmy did not do well in school. His teachers claimed he was "slow," which infuriated his mother. "He ain't dumb, you just ain't smart enough to teach him," she would say. But none of the teachers cared much for the rantings of a Cranston widow with a slow gnome for a son. And the counselors and therapists and educational bureaucrats were simply too overworked or too lazy or too full of apathy to notice that Timothy Navel was dyslexic.

In the second grade Tim was asked to write his name on the chalkboard. It came out "Mit." That recess three boys taunted

Tim mercilessly. Tim punched them all until they bled, and was sent home from school for his trouble. The name stuck.

With such humble, indeed humiliating, beginnings, Mitty was clearly not destined for success in the classroom. But he was strong, and tough, and he liked to be on his own. At seventeen he dropped out of Cranston East and bought a leaky plywood boat with a flat bottom and a greasy outboard. Armed with a steel bull rake and two plastic buckets, Mitty made his way in the world, scraping the bottom of Narragansett Bay for the succulent mollusks known as clams.

Mitt Navel prided himself on being a quahogger, the name given to those who hauled clams or "quahogs" from the ocean floor. He was not just a quahogger, he was a professional quahogger. A renegade professional quahogger. Mitty loved to work in the nether world of shellfishing, humping and dumping for all he was worth in the creeks and coves declared off-limits by the Rhode Island Department of Environmental Management. The shallow regions of the Bay were restricted in part to protect the quahog population, but also because parts of the Bay remained polluted. To unsuspecting diners, the clams could be deadly. To renegades like Mitty, they were gold.

Hard work and the cover of darkness paid off. Mitty harvested tens of thousands of clams, sometimes clearing eight or nine hundred dollars for a single night's load. He used the money to buy twin Mercury engines that he bolted on the stern of a bigger skiff that didn't leak as much, all the better to stay one step ahead of the cops.

At twenty-three, Mitty stood just four-eleven. He weighed close to 180, and had the appearance of a small ape. His hair was thick and stiff, and his beard grew in dark wisps off the sides of his face. Up close, it looked like he glued tiny bales of hay to his cheeks. Mitty's arms were powerful and long, hanging halfway to his knees. Privately, the men in the bars of Pawtuxet Village and Oakland Beach called him the troll. But none ever picked a fight. It would be suicide, all agreed, to mess with Mitty Navel.

He could feel the ebb tide pulling the skiff along, and when he passed a buoy that marked the entry to Pawtuxet Cove, he pulled the oars in and fired up the engines. He pushed them just past idle, navigating by feel, by instinct as he headed north.

Mitty didn't hate the DEM police who made his work more difficult. They were part of the challenge, what made quahogging an interesting line of work. But Mitty had no use for divers.

He hated them all, with their fancy rubber suits and plastic boats and tanks and red flags. Divers screwed up the clam beds, aggravated the quahogs that fetched ten dollars a bushel, and the little cherrystones that sold for forty or fifty.

Once, Mitty cut the line on a diver's flag buoy, then watched for an hour as two ski boats cut back and forth, scaring the poor diver half to death, making him afraid to come to the surface for fear of being hit or, worse, cut in two. Mitty thought it was funny when the bastard nearly drowned. Another time he deliberately drove his skiff over the anchor chain on a diver's boat, so the guy had to chase the drifting craft or swim a mile to shore with a tank and a weight belt.

But that was just for fun. This trip was business. The diver in question was mucking about in Mitty's personal clam bed, and it was time to pay.

There was no one else on the water at this hour, though Mitty could now see the winking lights from the shipping terminals up in Providence. There was no sign of other quahoggers on the water. His boat hummed along nicely, not too loud, cutting a slender, phosphorescent wake in the darkness.

After five or six minutes he cut the engine and listened to the motor die quietly. Then he grabbed his oars again and heaved away. He was getting close now, and after a few more minutes he began looking over his shoulder. There, perhaps fifty yards away, a white Boston Whaler emerged from the blackness. There was no dive flag, but fancy boats like this were rarely left anchored and unattended. Besides, Mitty had watched the boat for two nights now, silently cursing as he watched the diver roll over the side and down into his precious quahogs.

In a moment he was alongside. He shipped his oars and peered into the boat. He could barely make out a life preserver and a couple of buckets near the bow. They were empty. But back near the engine console, there was something else. A clipboard, covered in plastic. Words appeared on the clipboard, but it was too dark to read them.

Mitty held on to the side of the skiff. What he saw made him all the more angry, though he was not precisely sure why. Not only was this diver messing with the clams, but he was writing shit down while he did it. What for?

He grabbed the clipboard and tucked it inside the little cabin house at the back of his skiff. Then he reached for the box.

The materials came from a marine contractor who helped to build a fancy waterfront bar up the bay. The owner paid the guy to build a set of heavy-duty slips to accommodate big power cruisers, so they could park their boats safely while drinking fruity drinks and watching buxom women compete in the "Hot Bod" contests on summer afternoons. Of course, heavy-duty slips required breaking through the rocks twenty feet below the surface, to make room for pilings. And breaking through the rocks sometimes required the strategic use of dynamite.

The sticks were small, and Mitty wondered why he had not noticed this earlier when he lifted them from the contractor's supply shed. But it didn't matter. After all, he wasn't planning to kill the guy.

Mitty crammed a blasting cap into the top of a stick, then pinched on a fuse with a set of needlenose pliers. According to the pamphlet he'd purchased at an underground store in Cranston, that was all he needed to do. It took three hours of reading, and he had to go slow and make sure he understood each word. But using dynamite didn't seem all that hard.

A splash broke his concentration. Mitty turned to see an arm coming out of the water. Then a head. Damn, Mitty thought. This spoils the surprise.

He set the stick of dynamite down and reached for his bullrake. Just as the diver reached up to put a hand on the Whaler, Mitty dropped the rake on his head. The diver made a noise that sounded like a gurgle, then dropped briefly below the surface. A moment later he popped up again, and Mitty bashed him once more.

The diver sank below the surface again. Mitty dug into his jeans and found a Bic lighter. He'd hoped to take more time with the process, but he didn't want to hit the diver again. The rake was heavy, and after all, he only wanted to scare the guy.

The sky changed from black to deep purple, the first sign that morning was coming. Mitty reached for the stick once more, lit the fuse, and tossed the dynamite. It skipped across the water, then sank some thirty feet away. Mitty watched it slip below the surface, the burning fuse fading like an aging firefly. Then he started his engine.

He hadn't gone more than a hundred feet when the water behind him erupted. Mitty turned to see a black plume, perhaps the size of a two-story house. Then came the concussion, muted but still powerful, pushing his boat like a wave washing away a piece of driftwood. Mitty turned his back and roared down the bay, confident that the diver would think twice about messing with Mitty's clams again.

2

M ichael, I'm going home."
         Michael Carolina heard the words before he felt her
         shaking him.
         "Michael, wake up, I'm going."
Carolina rolled over and opened his eyes. Marie was sitting on
the edge of the bed, legs crossed, wearing a pair of jeans and a
University of Rhode Island sweatshirt. The first rays of the morning sun were creeping past the drawn shade, and lit the pale blue
lettering. As always, she looked supremely beautiful, and he
would have said so, but her words distracted him.

"Michael, I'm *going*."

"I heard you. What time is it?"

"Almost six A.M."

He sat up. She was looking at him, sad-eyed.

"Am I to assume this is a permanent thing?"

"It's permanent," Marie said.

"What happened?"

"Nothing. We're just not—right."

"What does that mean?"

"I don't know."

It was hard to believe, Carolina thought. They had been together a couple of months, long enough to enjoy one another's
company in bed, not nearly long enough to make any kind of serious commitment. Still, I like this lady, Carolina said to himself.
She was smart, tough, and self-assured, attributes that served her
well defending clients, many of them accused of rape or murder
or worse. And she was a beautiful woman, the kind that made

other women cringe or slip a protective arm around a boyfriend or husband when she walked into a party.

Marie got up and walked across the room. Carolina noticed her bag, already packed.

"How long have you been up?"

"A few hours."

"You work fast."

The phone rang. The sound was irritating, Carolina thought. Marie did not move. Carolina picked up after the third ring.

"H'lo?"

"Good morning," Shirley Templeton said. "We've got an explosion."

"Oh."

Shirley Templeton was news director at Channel Three, and the only news director Michael Carolina had ever truly respected.

"What kind of explosion?" he asked.

"I should go," Marie said, picking up her bag.

"Wait," Carolina said.

"It's on the waterfront in Edgewood. Am I interrupting something?" Shirley asked.

"Nothing much. I'm getting dumped," Carolina said. Marie was moving toward the door.

"Excuse me?" Shirley said.

"Hold on." Carolina put the phone down. "Marie—"

Marie Brine stopped.

"Nothing," she said. "It's not you. It's me."

"I think I deserve better than this."

"You do. You're a great guy, Michael. But I can't give you what you need."

"Either that or you won't," he replied. The moment the remark came out it embarrassed him, made him wonder if he sounded like a pouting child.

If his words had any impact, Marie gave no sign. She was out the door. For a moment he listened to her feet hitting the stairs outside the apartment. Then he picked up the phone again.

"Like I was saying," Shirley said, "we have a breaking news story and every second counts. But take your time."

"I'm sorry."

"What's going on?"

"Nothing. Really, nothing. Where's the explosion again?"

"Edgewood. On the waterfront. I need you down there right away."

"Anyone hurt?"

"We're not sure. The scanner had police calling for a rescue to stand by. I don't know anything more than that."

"Where's Edgewood?"

"Cranston. It's a pretty little neighborhood. Lots of nice houses."

"I hate houses," Carolina said, looking around. "I hate them only slightly less than apartments."

"Edgewood also has two yacht clubs," Shirley said.

"Then it has some redeeming qualities."

"Indeed. I want a live shot at seven twenty-five. Can you make it?"

Carolina stood up, letting the cradle of the phone dangle loosely, twisting by its cord and swinging just inches from the floor. He looked around the room. The place was in typical morning disarray, with his shirt and tie tossed loosely over a chair, an old pair of chinos peeking out beneath them. A pair of Docksides, one with its sole facing the ceiling, were spread between the chair and the door, in the same spots where he'd kicked them off the night before. He gazed across the dresser table, looking for the black leather band of the quartz wristwatch he'd slipped off before climbing into bed. It was still there, and he leaned over to pick it up when he noticed himself in the mirror.

He was thirty-five, dressed in baggy blue boxer shorts. I'm in reasonably decent shape, he thought to himself, noticing the lack of a paunch and realizing that all those hours of sailing had kept him more fit than most men his age. He couldn't remember the last time he weighed himself, but guessed he was no more than

165, not bad for a man who stood five-nine. His skin was tan, in deference to his Italian father and in total denial of the fairness he remembered in his Irish mother. *You're no perfect guy, Michael,* an old girlfriend had told him once, *but you'll definitely do.*

Still, at this hour of the morning, there was no denying he was a mess, his thick, dark hair shooting out wildly after a full night of sleep. A day's growth of beard was still sprouting along his jaw and chin, and when he yawned he realized his mouth tasted like a piece of burnt rubber. The sight in the mirror forced a wry smile to his face.

"What's not to love?" he murmured.

"Excuse me?" Shirley asked. He realized her patience had disappeared.

"How do I get there?"

"I'll have Earl pick you up."

"Why are you calling me instead of the assignment editor?"

"Because he didn't know who to send, and frankly, I think he's scared of you."

Carolina smiled. "Thanks."

"It wasn't a compliment. *I'm* not scared of you."

"Well," Carolina said. "I'll have to work on that."

"Michael."

"Yeah?"

"What did you mean about getting dumped?"

"I was just kidding."

Shirley hung up. Carolina looked around.

What am I doing here?

The apartment was a second-floor walk-up, nestled inside a Victorian home on Providence's East Side. The owner, an architect, used the first floor for offices, and renovated the upstairs to allow for tenants. For the sum of seven hundred a month, Carolina had a one-bedroom apartment with a fireplace and a new kitchen. *Very, very nice,* Marie said when she helped him move in.

But it did not feel like home.

Home had been a sailboat for the better part of the last five years. Carolina chartered a wooden boat in the Caribbean, and later in New England. The boat had been lost on his first visit to Rhode Island, when Shirley had hired him as an investigative reporter. The loss made Carolina restless, and when an insurance settlement came through he bought another boat, a pilot sloop, and set out to sea again. He had sailed as far as Tahiti before Shirley called, begging him to come back to investigate the death of a Channel Three colleague.

This time, he'd decided, Rhode Island had taken hold and wouldn't let go. He loved Providence, with its federalist architecture and magnificent restaurants and its rugged politics and neighborhoods. He loved the pride people had for their little state, the sense of community you could find in a working-class district in Pawtucket, or the tony section of Barrington or Bristol. He liked the lazy beaches in Newport, and the way that the bay and the ocean beckoned from the docks in East Providence. Rhode Island, he could feel, had crept into his blood, settled into his bones.

It was time to settle down, he had decided, and this was as good a place to be as any. Better, even, if you liked to sail and worked as a reporter by trade. Still, something was missing.

He tried not to think about it as he showered and dressed. But it was still there, strange and unsettling, in the back of his mind. He tried to imagine what it must be like for a young seminarian, or a convict getting used to the way things worked in prison. When he realized the depth of his self-pity, it was as if someone slapped him in the face.

"I've got to stop all this weirdness," he muttered to himself.

In a few minutes there was a horn outside. He walked out the door to see Earl Taylor, Channel Three's senior photographer, parked on the curb.

"Rise and shine, babe," Earl said happily.

Carolina grunted.

"What's the matter, you're not happy to see me?"

"I hear that as people get older, they enjoy getting up in the morning."

Earl laughed. "You're just jealous 'cause I'm so cheerful."

"That's it."

The photographer had been with Channel Three for over thirty years. He drove easily through Providence, down to Wickenden Street, across the Point Street Bridge, and eventually onto Allens Avenue, heading south toward Cranston.

"Rough night?" he asked Carolina.

"I'm just not a morning person."

"Well, this ought to wake you up."

Allens Avenue turned into Narragansett Boulevard. A string of commercial buildings and small stores quickly turned into houses and streets lined with trees and neatly trimmed shrubs. To his left Carolina caught glimpses of water behind the houses and yards, until finally Earl's van slipped down a hill and around one of the prettiest little harbors Carolina had ever seen. The view was marred by a string of police and rescue vehicles parked along the roadside, their strobes flashing in the early morning light.

"Stillhouse Cove," Earl said. "Never seen it so busy."

A Cranston officer stepped in front of the new van. The officer shot a finger at the van, then swept it toward a side street in the way policemen do when trying to keep a crazed situation under control. Earl followed the directions with a smile.

"Thanks, asshole," he said, then mumbled, "I hate when that happens."

"Don't get upset. It's a good sign," Carolina said.

"How's that?"

"What's the first thing a cop is trained to do when a situation is crazy?"

Earl looked at him for a moment. "Get things under control?"

"That's right. And when do police officers most feel the need to get things under control?"

It was almost as if a light went on in the old photographer's head. "When they don't know what's going on?"

Now Carolina smiled.

"So you think the story's still hot?"

"What I think," Carolina said, "is we need to move our respective asses."

They found a spot half a block from where the cop was standing. Earl punched a button on the van's hatch. In a moment he had his camera on his shoulder. Carolina was already halfway down the street. The two of them jogged toward the cove.

Carolina heard a shout, and looked out at the water. There were two police boats, one at full stop, one easing past it. The stopped boat had a diver in the water and two men standing by to help him. The diver was trying to push a body into the boat.

"Earl," Carolina said.

"I'm rolling," came the reply.

In a moment the body was in the boat. It looked to Carolina like another diver, but the two men who had pulled the man aboard quickly blocked his view. Then a third man, the boat's pilot, slipped his engine into gear, and the little craft sped toward the docks at the Rhode Island Yacht Club.

"Good shit," Earl said. "Really good shit."

Stillhouse Cove was ringed with houses. A few people appeared on porches and lawns, disturbed by the commotion below. Earl turned to get a shot of them, making long, steady sweeps with his camera. Then reporter and photographer started walking toward the yacht club, a wooden building stained bluish-gray and perched at the water's edge.

"Nice place to keep your boat," Earl said. In fact, the club's marina was littered with expensive-looking vessels, bobbing gently.

But there was no time to look at them. The club entrance was still a good quarter mile away. Before they reached the gate, the air was pierced with the sound of a rescue siren. Earl stopped running, leveled his camera, and aimed toward the gate. In a moment, a rescue truck shot through the gate, then rolled past, screaming all the way as it headed toward Ocean State Hospital.

"We need sound," Carolina said.

They walked through the gate of the club. In the parking lot and down on the docks, confusion reigned. Two divers—policemen, judging from the lettering on their wet suits—were talking to two men in plainclothes. Another group of men stared out at the cove, pointing. When Carolina saw what they were looking at he stopped short.

It was a Boston Whaler, upside down. But the boat was not in the water. Instead it lay impaled on a piling, skewered like a chicken on a stick.

"Earl," Carolina said.

"What? Oh, fuck. I mean *really, really, really good shit.*"

The plainclothes officers had left the divers now. One of them walked toward the boat, pulling out a small still camera to take some photographs of his own.

"We still need some sound," Carolina muttered.

"Go find someone," Earl said. "You know where to find me."

Carolina started to walk around. Cranston cops, he thought to himself, I don't know any Cranston cops.

Carolina set his sights on a slender officer who appeared to be in his early fifties. The man spoke into a police radio from time to time. He had the look of authority.

"Excuse me, officer." The man looked at him. "I'm Michael Carolina, Channel Three."

"I don't have time to talk right now," the man said. He turned to speak into the radio. "This is Franco. Has anybody raised ATF yet?"

"We're working on it, Captain," a female voice replied.

"Who are they sending?"

"We don't know." The female dispatcher sounded aggravated. The slender officer swore silently.

"My guess," Carolina said, "is they'll send Bert Schumacher and Ernie O'Mara."

The cop looked up.

"That is, unless they've been transferred, Captain."

"And how would you know, Mr.—?"

"Carolina. Michael Carolina. I've met them before."

"Really?"

"Yes. On another boat explosion."

"I see. You specialize in this sort of story?"

"Actually this is my first."

The cop began to look irritated. "I thought you met two ATF agents when another boat was blown up."

"I did."

"So you just hang around watching ships go up for fun?"

"No, the last time someone blew up my boat."

The policeman paused for a second. Carolina looked around. Earl was still rolling tape on the spiked Whaler. Some other TV crew was arriving in the area. Out by the road, traffic was picking up with morning rush hour.

The policeman extended his hand. "I'm Jack Franco."

Carolina shook.

"You know," Franco said, "I think I remember this. Was it in Warwick? One of the marinas?"

"That's it."

"You know who did it?"

"Yeah."

"Would he have been available to do this?"

"I doubt it. He's dead."

Franco paused again. Carolina looked up once more to see two familiar figures making their way toward the dock.

"Listen, Captain, I could really use a little help here. What happened?"

"Well," Franco said. "We got a call about an hour ago. The noise woke up everyone in the neighborhood, I guess. We got here, that boat was on the piling, there, and the water's still. We looked around, found some gear, decided to check the water."

"Who'd you find?" The two figures were getting closer.

"Some guy. Had a diving suit on. One of my people said he was down at the bottom of the cove."

"Really? He still alive?"

"Had a pulse, I understand. I guess there was enough oxygen—"

"Captain," a voice cut in.

"Hello, Bert. Hello, Ernie." Carolina said.

The younger agent, Ernie O'Mara, glared at the reporter. The other one sighed and nodded as Franco doubled over with laughter.

"Captain, meet Mr. Schumacher and Mr. O'Mara."

When Franco recovered, he shook hands with the two ATF men.

"Watch out for this guy," Ernie said. "He's trouble."

"Is that any way to treat a friend?" Carolina asked.

"You're a reporter," Bert said, showing the first signs of a grin. "You guys don't have friends."

"I take it you people have some history?" Franco asked.

Bert and Ernie nodded. "In a manner of speaking," Carolina said. "Captain, I wonder if we could do a quick interview about the status of things. I've got to do a piece for seven twenty-five."

The two ATF agents frowned. They didn't want a local cop giving interviews before talking to them. Franco noticed.

"I'd like to help you, Mike," the captain said. "But I've got to confer with my colleagues here."

Ernie O'Mara looked positively smug.

"Well," Carolina said. "Thanks for the cooperation."

"Come back later," Franco called as Carolina walked back up the dock. "I'll try and get you something."

"No dice?" Earl asked when he reached the pier's end. Carolina shook his head. "The Sesame Street kids have long memories."

Other crews were gathered along the shore of the cove now, shooting tape of the waterfront and the broken Whaler sticking up from the piling.

"Don't worry," Earl said. "We've got the best shit. Bet you didn't even see that."

The photographer was looking at a diver who was wrestling a

large piece of wood into one of the police boats. The piece was sculpted and curved, like part of a ship's wooden frame.

"I got a bunch of stuff like that," Earl said. "Wonder what the pieces came from."

In the distance, a Channel Three microwave truck rolled into view. Earl and Carolina started to walk back to feed tape. They approached a state vehicle with the letters "DEM" on the side. Department of Environmental Management. A uniformed officer stood in front, arms crossed, hip cocked, hat raked, khaki uniform crisp. Kind of small for a cop, Carolina thought, squinting to get a better look at the man. Only then did he realize that it wasn't a man at all, but a very tanned attractive young woman.

Carolina followed the officer's gaze, and realized it was directed toward the Cranston police captain and the two federal agents. This was her turf, he realized, her jurisdiction, but the male officers seemed to be ignoring her. The DEM officer kept staring at them, saying nothing. As Carolina passed, the officer turned to look at him, then back at the men on the marina docks.

She looked sad, he decided, very sad indeed.

The realtor was disturbed by what she saw. The TV screen was filled with images of police boats and divers hauling pieces of wood from the bottom of the cove. Worse still was the picture of the broken man being pulled aboard the boat, the victim of what the TV guy said was a mysterious bombing.

It all made her nervous. The realtor hugged herself. Though it was mid-June and the temperature was already easing into the high seventies, she was cold. She was always cold. She reached for another cigarette, lit up, and dragged deeply, as if the smoke would help to warm her up.

But she was still nervous.

She reached for the telephone and dialed the special number that would connect her with Jimmy Flannery.

"What?" a voice answered.

"I'm watching the news. You watching the news?"

"This better be fucking good," the voice said. She hated to make Flannery upset. Few people had ever genuinely frightened her, but Jimmy Flannery was one of them.

"Channel Three," she said. "Try Channel Three."

She listened to Flannery exhale as he reached for the television remote, then punched buttons. In the background she could hear the sound of Katie Couric flirting with Al Roker or some other NBC guy. Then, from the sound, she could tell Flannery had switched to Channel Three.

"The fuck is this?" Flannery said.

"That's our meal ticket," the realtor said, and took another drag. "They blew up the diver."

"What? Who blew up the diver?"

"How should I know, Jimmy? The report says he got blown up. They had tape of him being taken to the hospital."

Flannery fell silent. The realtor hated this even more than when Jimmy swore. When Jimmy Flannery grew quiet, bad things could happen.

"So what does this do to us?" he asked.

"I don't know."

"You know," Jimmy said. "This could be good."

The realtor didn't know what Jimmy was talking about.

"I mean, bombs in the hood don't exactly do wonders for real estate prices," he said.

The realtor hugged herself again. She realized that he had a point. But it didn't make her feel better.

"We still don't know who's responsible."

"Don't worry about that," Jimmy said. "I'll take care of that."

"And we don't know what happened with the diver. He could be talking to people."

"Didn't youse used to work in a nursing home?"

The realtor sighed. She'd held a lot of jobs, at one time or another.

"Yeah," Jimmy said. "I thought you did. So that's your job. Find out what's going on and let me know."

Flannery hung up.

The realtor finished her cigarette. The reporter had thrown back to the anchor, and now the anchor was chatting happily with a weather guy about what a swell day it was going to be. She shut the television off, wondering where she could get a cheap nurse's uniform. She still felt cold.

"Nice job," Shirley said. "The cut-in looked great. How come you didn't have any sound?"

"Two friends of mine from ATF persuaded a certain Cranston police captain not to."

"That fat guy and the skinny kid thinks he's J. Edgar Hoover?"

"The same."

"I didn't think they were still working around here."

Carolina looked out at the cove again. The local affiliate camera crews were in full swing, photographers running around looking for pictures, reporters desperately trying to wring information out of anyone with a pulse. A crew from a regional cable station was just pulling in, always the last to arrive. Carolina smiled as he watched a young woman scream at her photographer to get his ass moving. She practically tackled a man in his bathrobe, asking him what was going on.

"I wanted you to cover the casino rally at the State House," Shirley was saying, "but why don't you stick with this."

"I can't believe they're pushing gambling as a way to make money."

"Hey, everybody's doing it. Connecticut. Up in Massachusetts. No one wants to get left behind. Besides, since the General Assembly passed the referendum bill, this has turned into a hot topic."

"I know. I just think the whole revenue thing is bullshit."

"Maybe it is, but the voters will have to decide."

Carolina didn't answer. The thought of gambling, particularly the organized kind, sickened him.

"Hello?" Shirley said. "You still with me?"

"Yeah."

"Is something wrong?"

"Why do you say that?"

"I don't know," Shirley said. "I always talk to my reporters and have them drift off in the middle."

"Sorry."

"Not a problem. Listen, I'd love to continue discussing public policy, but I think you have some work to do. The way things look, you've got the lead tonight."

"Yes, boss."

Carolina hung up the cell phone. The man in the bathrobe was waving his arms at the cable reporter and telling her for the third time that no, he didn't know what happened, and he didn't want to be on television. The reporter refused to take the hint, and finally the man stormed back into his house, the belt of his robe flapping behind him. Carolina watched as he disappeared into a Queen Anne Victorian. The house had a magnificent view of the waterfront. Carolina almost missed the SOLD sign slapped on top of the real estate placard that read WHIPPLE REALTY in front of the building.

Half an hour later, Captain Franco agreed to an interview. No less than five cameras—three from Providence, one from the cable station, and one from a network affiliate from Boston—surrounded him. Pelted with questions from all sides, interrupted every third or fourth syllable, Franco eventually shook his head in disgust and walked away.

"This is not good," Carolina said.

"We don't have shit for sound," Earl agreed.

There are two important elements to a great television news story. One is great pictures, and this is the element producers crave the most. The other is sound, the quotes that set a story's pace and, hopefully, provide information and drama. A "package," or taped story, can be done without sound or it can be done with only a few pictures. The goal of any television reporter, however, is to get the best of both.

With the video of the injured man, the ambulance roaring off to the hospital, and the graphic image of the broken Boston Whaler, Channel Three had more than enough video. But Carolina knew they still needed more.

"I've got an idea," he said.

"Would you like to share it?" Earl asked.

"In a minute. Let's go back to the van."

"Why? We're leaving?"

"Yeah. I need to find a pay phone."

"Ocean State Hospital."

"Yes, this is Captain Franco, Cranston police. Emergency room, please."

"Emergency."

"Yes, Captain Franco, Cranston police. We'd like to ask some questions of that diver you received from Edgewood. Let's see, did the EMTs find any ID on him?"

"The bombing victim? Don't think so. He's admitted as a John Doe."

"I see. What's his condition?"

"Stable. But you'll have trouble talking to him."

"Why's that?"

"We think the blast ruptured his eardrums."

"That's too bad," Carolina said. "Do you have him in a room yet?" The nurse gave him the number.

"I can't believe you did that," Earl said.

Carolina cocked an eyebrow.

"We're just getting started."

3

Ocean State Hospital is the largest and perhaps the finest general medical facility in Rhode Island. It sits in a sort of medical ghetto on the border of downtown and South Providence, between a children's hospital, a maternity hospital, and a crop of office buildings for doctors, therapists, and anyone else connected with the business of health care. Ocean State is a teaching hospital, and has both excellent staff and equipment.

Despite the stature of the institution, the people who run the hospital are notoriously paranoid. The security force reacts to trouble with all the grace and precision of Nazi storm troopers. The public relations division rules the local media with an iron fist, rewarding those who report the hospital party line, and punishing anyone who dares to question a policy or rule.

Michael Carolina was not familiar with Ocean State Hospital. It didn't matter. In his experience he had never found a hospital that wasn't loaded with obnoxious security guards and public relations flaks who felt their primary job was to obstruct reporters as much as humanly possible. There was simply no way to convince people employed by a hospital that you should be permitted to do your job. And that, Carolina knew, left just one alternative.

Ignore them.

"I've been shooting film and tape for thirty years," Earl said. "But never in a bathrobe."

"Trust me," Carolina said.

"You sure Shirley will back you up for the wheelchair rental?"

"She will," Carolina said. "As long as I get what I'm looking for."

"Then why didn't you call to get her okay?"

"There are some things bosses don't want to know about."

They parked in a public lot behind the building's rear entrance. Carolina slid open the van's side door and set the wheelchair down. Earl climbed in, tucking his camera under a blanket.

"There's no easy way for me to say this," Carolina said. Earl looked at him.

"Your pants are showing."

"So?" Earl said.

Carolina said nothing.

"Forget it, Mike. I'll sneak into the place with you. I'll help you look for the guy who got hurt, and I'll tape an interview if we can get it. But there's no fucking way I'm taking off my pants so you can get a sound bite."

"Well, could you at least roll the legs up?"

Earl did, revealing white, spindly calves sticking out above a pair of old slippers.

"I can't believe I'm doing this," Earl muttered.

They crossed the street. Carolina rolled the chair up the sidewalk and into what looked like a garden near the rear entrance. After a moment they noticed a nurse pushing another patient in a chair.

"This is good," Carolina said. "We'll blend right in."

Earl shifted in the chair. "I feel sick already."

They lingered for a moment, looking around, then slipped inside the building. No guard was posted at the rear entrance. There was a waiting area, filled with chairs and a television set tuned to a late-morning soap opera. The few people watching did not look up.

"Where is he again?" Earl whispered.

"Fifth floor, west side. Let me find some elevators."

A moment later they found a bank of four. There were more

people moving around now, mostly nurses and orderlies, with a few doctors mixed in. No one paid them any attention.

"Camera's digging into my side," Earl grumbled.

"You can handle it," Carolina said, smiling at a nurse who did not smile back.

"Easy for you to say."

It took another five minutes to find the room. The man identified by the ER nurse as the bombing victim was in a four-bed ward. Carolina rolled Earl past the door, sneaking a look inside. He sighed. Three of the beds looked empty. A pair of legs stuck out of the one closest to the door.

"Looks okay," he said. "If he's in there he's the only one."

Earl nodded. "Let's move it. The battery's cutting off my circulation."

The room smelled strongly of disinfectant and the smell of new paint. The three empty beds lay flat and neatly made, ready for new arrivals. An air-conditioning unit hummed quietly, wrapped in a metal casing that ran the length of the window.

Carolina wheeled the chair to face the occupied bed.

It was hard to tell, but Carolina guessed the patient was in his mid-thirties and swarthy. An IV unit dripped clear liquid into his left arm, while some sort of machine seemed to measure his heart rate. The only other sign that he'd been injured was the gauze bandages wrapped turban style around the man's head.

And he was wide awake.

"Ahem," Carolina said.

The man stared at him, but made no sign.

"Great opening," Earl mumbled.

"How are you?" Carolina asked.

The patient continued to stare.

"Didn't you say his eardrums blew out?" Earl asked.

Carolina felt his face turning beet red. All the way up here, all this risk, and he had not thought about how to talk to the man.

"Jesus, do I have to think of everything?" From inside his robe

Earl fished out a small notepad, then a pen. He handed them over. Carolina quickly scribbled HOW ARE YOU? and held the pad up.

The man still appeared a little woozy. But after a moment he said, "Who are you?"

A chart lay at the end of the bed. Someone had scrawled "dem" under a column for medications, and a dosage amount.

I'M A REPORTER, Carolina wrote on the notepad. WHAT'S YOUR NAME?

The man closed his eyes. Carolina thought he was trying to smile, but it turned into a grimace.

"Tony," he whispered. Carolina waited.

Carolina scribbled down the name. He wrote WHAT HAPPENED? and held up his pad.

The man took a moment to focus again. Earl was struggling with his camera, finally pulling it completely out from under his robe.

"Ahh," Earl said, relieved.

The man was staring at the notepad. Carolina thought he might as well have been looking at a wall.

The man said, "Big bang, baby. Big bang."

"Wonderful," Earl said. "Real insight."

There was noise from the hallway. Carolina wrote, WHAT WERE YOU DOING IN THE COVE?

The man tried to focus again. The voices were getting louder. The man made a honking noise. For a moment Carolina thought he was choking, and then he caught the tone. The man was laughing, or trying to, hovering between mirth and pain. He waved an arm for a moment, and Carolina noticed a detailed tattoo of an anchor, along with a line of red marks up to the elbow.

Then Carolina realized what the man was doing with his arm. He was shaking his hand, flicking his wrist, and opening his fingers. Shake and throw.

"Gotta roll the dice baby. Just roll the dice."

"What are you doing here?"

Carolina turned. A very angry woman with a stethoscope around her neck was standing in the door.

"We were talking."

"Roll them dice, babe," Tony said.

"And who are you?" the woman demanded. She wore a badge that read RN.

"Uh, hospital public affairs," Carolina said.

"We're working on a special," Earl added. "It's called Bombing and Demerol: the Winning Combination."

"Don't move," the nurse said.

"Sorry, we're on a deadline," Carolina said, wheeling the chair. He rammed the chair forward and the nurse jumped.

"Roll the dice, babe," the man said behind them.

They were rolling down the hall now.

"Did you get it?" Carolina asked.

Earl snapped a look at him. "Of course. Just get us out of here."

They hit the elevator bank just as one opened. It took all of Carolina's strength to slow the momentum of the chair. They barely missed a patient being wheeled on a gurney. The orderly pushing the gurney narrowed his eyes.

"Watch your speed, man."

"Sorry," Carolina said.

As the doors were closing, Carolina and Earl saw the RN rounding the corner with a security guard in tow.

"Shit," Earl said.

The doors closed before the guard could reach them. The elevator started to move.

"We're going up," Earl said.

"Thanks for noticing," Carolina answered.

"That means we're fucked."

"Ditch the robe," Carolina said. "And never say die."

The car stopped on the seventh floor. There was no one there to greet them when the doors opened.

Earl said, "What now?"

"Stay calm. Act like you know what you're doing."

"Oh. Sure." Earl rolled his eyes.

They set off down the hall, Carolina looking in every door, Earl carrying his camera like a suitcase. Both moved straight ahead, and no one seemed to pay attention.

They turned a corner. A security man in a blue blazer was ten feet away, standing at a nursing station. The man was speaking into a radio. His back was turned.

Across the hall was a room marked SUPPLY. Carolina pointed. Earl stepped over and tried the door. It opened. They slipped inside.

"We need to split up," Carolina said.

Earl nodded. He punched the EJECT button on the Betacam. In a moment the camera spit out a cassette, and Earl handed it to his reporter. Carolina stuffed the cassette into his belt.

"It'll be easier for you to get out of here," Earl said. Then he pointed to the camera. "But this is worth forty grand. I can't leave it. And I might as well wear a sign if I carry it."

Carolina looked around. The room was loaded with linens and towels. And several boxes of toilet pap.er.

Carolina walked out of the hospital five minutes later. He took a long walk through the garden, then sauntered over to the news van. Earl had not arrived. Carolina hit the alarm key and the van chirped as the doors unlocked. He climbed into the driver's seat, popped the cassette into a box, and dropped it on the seat beside him.

Three minutes later he spotted Earl coming down the street that led to Ocean State Hospital's emergency entrance. Earl walked quickly, his head sweeping back and forth to see if anyone was watching or following. He carried a large box marked TOILET TISSUE, INDUSTRIAL SIZE.

"Someone's gonna think I'm stealing this," he said, climbing into the van.

"Nah," Carolina said. "And even if they did, it probably happens all the time."

Carolina started the engine as Earl wedged himself into the front seat.

The van eased through the parking lot, toward the entrance that would take them to Eddy Street, then back downtown.

"Well," Earl said, "that was pretty strange. But I guess we made it—oh, shit."

"What?"

"We forgot the wheelchair."

Before Carolina could answer, the roar of a car engine pierced the air, followed by screeching tires. A blue Ford midsize came to a halt in front of the van. Carolina stomped on the brakes, almost throwing Earl from his seat as Ernie O'Mara jumped from the Ford, gun drawn, and pointed at Carolina's head.

"FREEZE, MOTHERFUCKERS, hands on the dash, or the roof of that van's gonna wear your brains."

Carolina said, "I think we'll discuss the wheelchair later."

4

Bert Schumacher scratched his head.

"Aw, for chrissake, Ernie, put your friggin' gun down."

"He's making a break," Ernie said. He did not drop his gun.

"The hell he was. He's a dumb-fuck reporter who snuck into the hospital. Now put your goddamned gun away before I shoot you myself."

The parking lot was starting to fill up with hospital security guards, all of them wild-eyed with the knowledge that ATF had assisted in nailing dangerous hospital infiltrators.

Bert Schumacher now looked genuinely irritated.

"Ernie, put the gun down!"

Ernie wavered. Then, slowly, he lowered the nine-millimeter to his side.

"Uuhh," Carolina said, feeling the air leaving his chest. He looked at Earl. The photographer's hands gripped the dash. He said nothing, but his knuckles were snow white.

Bert Schumacher was at the door, opening it. He reached inside, turned the ignition off, and grabbed the keys.

"Are you all right?"

Carolina's head was whirling.

"He could have killed me."

"Naw, just scared you a little," Bert said.

Ernie O'Mara had reholstered his weapon. He wore a look of malevolence as he stared at Carolina, but still managed to finger a pimple where his neck met the collar of his shirt.

"Listen, uh, what's your name again?" Bert asked.

"Carolina. Michael Carolina."

"Yeah, uh, listen, Mike. I'm sorry about this, but we kind of figured it was you when we walked in the hospital and saw their security going nuts."

The hospital security guards were inching toward the car, like dogs drawn to bleeding prey.

"Personally, I think you're kind of lucky you got stopped by us instead of them."

"We didn't do anything," Carolina said.

Special Agent Schumacher smiled.

"Let's see. For starters, trespassing on private property. Impersonating hospital personnel. And"—Schumacher looked at the box of toilet paper—"theft of hospital property."

"The box was empty," Earl said.

"How do I know that?" Schumacher countered.

"Take a look." Earl pulled the box up. "See? Just used it to cover my camera."

Carolina closed his eyes. Schumacher's smile broadened. "Gentlemen," the agent said. "There are two choices here: One, we take you back inside, call the Providence PD, and you miss your deadline tonight. The other is you hand over that tape."

"Forget it," Carolina said.

"Mike!" Earl said. The older photographer looked anxious.

"You should listen to your buddy, Mike," Schumacher said.

"If you'd let me get some sound with Franco this morning, we wouldn't have even tried to talk to the guy. Why don't you go talk to him yourself?"

"Because his doctor upped his meds. He's so wired on Demerol he won't be down for a week. What am I doing?" Schumacher looked irritated again. "I don't have to explain myself to you."

Ernie O'Mara now stood behind his partner.

"Don't waste your breath, Bert. Let's just take the tape."

Ernie reached inside the van. Carolina grabbed his arm and pushed it away. A scuffle began.

"Knock it off!" Bert cried.

Ernie backed away. "That's assault on a federal officer," he said, sounding hurt.

"Ernie, shut up and go sit in the car."

Carolina's face was red.

"ATF. You guys are all cowboys. I'm just trying to do my job."

"You shut up, too," Bert said. "Look, I know we made it tough on you. I know you don't like me, and frankly, I don't like reporters. But I need to see your goddamned tape. It may be the only lead I have right now."

"I'm not a cop," Carolina said.

"And I'm not a journalist," Bert answered. "But you can either help me out and drive away from here, or spend the next several hours explaining what happened to a bunch of very unsympathetic police officers."

Carolina thought for a moment. He looked at Earl. The photographer had regained some, though not all, of his composure.

"I bet you don't even have a machine to play it on," Earl said. Carolina got the hint.

"If you follow me back to my station," he said, "we'll play it for you on our machines. We'll even make you a dub."

Schumacher looked at him. "What's a dub?"

"A copy of the tape," Earl said.

At that moment a gray-suited man pushed his way through the crowd. "What's going on here? Who's in charge?"

The man was perhaps five-six, balding, and wearing a mustache that looked like it had been inked on his lip with a felt pen. He had the palest skin Carolina had ever seen.

"I'm Stuart Bleeder, hospital public affairs." Bleeder pointed at Carolina. "Who is this man?"

"This is Mr. Carolina from Channel Three."

"I want him arrested," Bleeder said. Carolina noticed that the pitch of the man's voice was exceptionally high, as if he had been neutered.

"For what?" Bert asked.

Bleeder swallowed, then fired a savage look at Carolina. "This man trespassed into the hospital. We have a nurse who can identify him. And his friend."

Ernie O'Mara had climbed back out of the car. He looked as if he wanted to say something, but a look from Bert stopped him.

"Mr. Bleeder," Bert said. "These men are witnesses in a federal investigation. And they're coming with me."

"You can't do that!" Bleeder cried. "I want these men arrested! Right now!"

Bleeder jumped up and down, thrashing his fists against his legs. The hospital guards, uncertain, were backing up, eyes shifting from Bleeder to Bert and back to Bleeder. The agents tried hard not to laugh.

Bert looked at Carolina. "You show it to us, and we get a copy, right?"

"Right," Carolina said.

"Deal." Bert winked.

"You can't do that!" Bleeder squealed. "You can't do that!"

"Mr. Bleeder," Bert said calmly. "I'm a federal agent. With all due respect, sir, I can do whatever the fuck I want."

Bert climbed into his car and moved it out of the way. The two agents followed the Channel Three van downtown.

"That was good work, Bert," Ernie said.

"Good cop, bad cop, works every time," Bert said. "But I'm worried about you."

"Why's that, Bert?"

"You act like you're in a Quentin Tarantino movie. Jesus, lighten up."

Ernie looked hurt. "I thought you wanted me to intimidate them."

"Yeah, but there's a limit."

"What'd I do wrong?"

"For one, kid, you don't throw down on every guy you stop."

"What else?"

"Don't get into a shoving match."

"Why not? He asked for it."

"Bullshit."

"I could take him," Ernie said, brimming with false confidence. Bert shook his head sadly. "Another minute by the van there, Ernie, that reporter would've kicked your ass."

Bert and Ernie spent an hour in an edit booth at Channel Three, looking at the tape over and over.

"I can't believe you made this deal," Shirley said. "We don't share tape with cops."

"We do if we're going to lose it," Carolina said.

Shirley thought for a minute. "I don't like it. But I wasn't there."

She said nothing else, and Carolina knew he had won the point. But Shirley wasn't finished.

"I would like a word with you about the methods you used to get access to the patient."

"Who, my buddy Tony?" Carolina said with a look of mock innocence.

"Yes," Shirley said with a grimace.

"All right."

"I received a call from a Mr. Bleeder. He was rather upset."

"I can imagine."

"Says you have violated the trust of the hospital."

"Yeah."

"Invaded a patient's privacy."

"I told the guy who I was."

"You infiltrated the leading hospital in this state in a wheelchair. You sneaked into a ward with your photographer in a bathrobe. You then told a heavily medicated man with punctured eardrums that you were a reporter."

Carolina folded his arms. "So what's your point?"

Shirley sighed. "Bleeder says you're banned from the hospital for life."

There was silence for a moment.

"That noise you hear is my heart breaking," Carolina said.

"If it was only you, Michael, I could live with it. But Bleeder says our reporters will never get a thing from them on any story in the future."

"Did we ever get anything before?"

"This is serious, Michael. Bleeder says you should have come to him first if you wanted to talk to the man."

"So he could stall us for five hours and then say no? You know better than that."

Shirley smiled. She reached for a bottle of vitamins and a cigarette.

"I can't believe you're still using those," Carolina said.

"Which?"

"Both."

"These," Shirley said, holding the vitamins, "keep me going. And this"—she paused to light up—"helps prevent me from strangling my employees."

Carolina smiled. "With all apologies to Nathan Hale, my only regret is that I didn't get more out of him."

Bert and Ernie appeared at the door of Shirley's office. Bert appeared ponderous, Ernie downright sullen.

"Doesn't say much, does he?" Bert said.

Carolina shrugged. "I didn't have a lot of time to break the ice."

"Should've let a professional handle it," Ernie muttered.

"Shut up, Ernie," Bert said, embarrassed.

"Oh, that's all right," Carolina said. "I'm sure Agent O'Mara here is a very skilled interviewer."

"Don't patronize me," Ernie said.

"You're right," Carolina said. "Why don't you kiss my ass?"

Ernie swelled with rage. Bert grabbed him.

"We'll be going," the older agent said, half dragging his partner out of the office.

"That was mature," Shirley said when the ATF men were gone.

"Sorry. The guy had me in his crosshairs. He wanted to shoot me."

"He's a federal agent?"

"He's an idiot."

Shirley looked down at Carolina. "Perhaps," she said. "You seem to know one when you see one."

The dig was a subtle one. Carolina looked at his boss, who now wore her own innocent expression.

"I guess you want me to write a story."

"Great idea," Shirley said.

He left her office, wrote a script, then spent an hour with an editor putting a piece together for the station's six o'clock. When he finished, he dialed a number.

"Law offices." Carolina recognized the voice of Marie's secretary.

"Hi, it's Michael Carolina."

"Hello." The woman's tone was cool. But then, it always had been.

"Is Marie in?"

"No."

"Can I leave a message?"

"Yes."

"Please just tell her I called." He left the station number.

The producer did not insist on a live shot from Stillhouse Cove, so Carolina watched his taped piece air from Shirley's office. They also scanned the competition.

"Nice job," she said as the sound bite with the bombing victim came on. "No one else got that."

"Too bad he didn't say more."

But Shirley wasn't listening. She turned the sound down on Carolina's piece and turned up Channel Nine. The competing station's reporter, a young man, was almost hyperventilating.

"Sources tell Channel Nine that the investigation into the explosion may have yielded a remarkable discovery."

The screen cut to a shot of the pieces of wood being lifted from the water.

"Those sources suspect that these remains of a wooden ship may actually belong to the HMS *Gaspee*."

"Oh, shit," Shirley groaned.

"What's he talking about?" Carolina asked. But Shirley was yelling for the night assignment editor, telling him to get a reporter.

The Channel Nine reporter now was interviewing a spokesman for a maritime historical society. The man was careful not to confirm anything, but said the society was "very interested in what had been found in the waters near Stillhouse Cove."

"What's the *Gaspee?*"

"A big piece of Rhode Island history," Shirley mumbled. The assignment editor poked his head in to say he was putting a night reporter on the story.

"I can work this if you want," Carolina said, but Shirley waved him off.

"You've worked long enough today already. Besides, I'm supposed to cut back on overtime."

"Sorry I didn't have it."

Shirley looked pained. She hated getting burned on a story. Any story.

"It's okay," she said. "You got something no one else did."

"Yeah, but it didn't add much to the story."

"Sure it did. I'll bet they're going crazy over at Nine and Thirteen."

Carolina said nothing for a moment. He looked back at the monitors. All three stations were now reporting the lesser stories of the day, including the rally at the Rhode Island State House. The rotunda was filled with demonstrators chanting in favor of the gambling referendum. One man held a sign that said CASINOS ARE A SURE THING. Another one read BET ON JOBS.

The pictures stirred memories Carolina preferred to forget. Of men knocking on a door to a house long ago. Repossession men, taking furniture and appliances, all under the watchful eye of a sheriff. Of angry phone calls late at night. A stunning, yet dignified woman, aging too rapidly, trying to hide tears. He blinked twice and looked down, then was almost grateful when he heard Shirley's voice again.

"So that lawyer broke up with you?"

"Yeah," Carolina said. He did not look at her.

"Why?"

"Your bet is as good as mine."

The unintended irony made him smile.

"I don't suppose that has anything to do with you being a little off your game today?"

"What do you mean?"

"Well, you know." Shirley looked at the floor. "You're a very aggressive reporter. That's why I hired you. And it's great that we got the stuff with the bombing victim. But sneaking into the hospital like that, that's kind of on the edge. And then getting beat on this *Gaspee* thing."

"Maybe you're right," Carolina said. "But you still haven't told me why the *Gaspee* is so important."

"It's a revolutionary war thing," Shirley said. "Bunch of locals burned a ship. I'm not familiar with all the details, but it's kind of important around here."

"I see."

They watched the end of the broadcast, and then a crew of people began to arrive in Shirley's office for a critique.

"I'm going to take off," Carolina said.

"Want to grab a bite later?" Shirley asked.

"Thanks," he said, "but I'm not hungry."

Carolina went back to his desk and picked up the phone. The line to Marie Brine's office rang and rang.

5

There were still several hours of light left when Carolina left the station. He walked up College Hill and over to Thayer Street, enjoying the quiet and the warm weather. The Brown students had disappeared for the summer, but the street was filled with panhandlers and high school kids, desperate to be free of adult supervision.

"Change for a samwitch, mista?" asked a heavyset lady in curlers, tank top, and flip-flops. The woman smoked absently while waiting for a response. Carolina kept walking.

He stopped into the College Hill and Brown bookstores to check out the titles. He stopped into a record shop, and thought about buying a Stone Temple Pilots album. Something about that tune "Interstate Love Song" pulled at him, made him think of cruising with the top down and the wind rushing past. But he fought back the urge to make a purchase.

It was a fine evening, warm and dry and clear, and Thayer Street was alive. Carolina thought about a movie and something to eat, maybe Indian food or something from that Tex-Mex place. Maybe a movie at the Avon. Anything to keep from going home.

He had first seen Marie in the spring, on a story he was covering in superior court. She was representing a convicted embezzler, and Carolina liked the way she handled herself, taking control of the courtroom, making her points, deflecting the arguments of prosecutors, dressing outrageously and managing to look drop-dead gorgeous all at the same time.

She was so good that he called her when he was in trouble himself. It was a minor charge: slugging another reporter who dearly needed it. Marie got the charge dropped, and in the course of doing so they both decided they were interested in one another. They spent the early summer sailing Marie's boat out to Prudence Island, drinking beer, and wrestling each other's clothes off in the cabin.

"You know," she said, after one extended bout on a Sunday afternoon, "I wonder about you."

"What do you wonder?"

"Whether you're a little too *normal.*"

"Excuse me?"

She looked sad for a moment, and then the look was gone. As he walked down the street, he thought about that moment in the cramped little cabin of her sailboat, and the way that she looked at him, and he realized it was the same look she wore that morning when she said she was going home.

He walked past a hot dog shop and an army-navy store and he would have kept his head down, thinking about Marie and what to do about getting something to eat, but the aroma of hot Thai food blasted him like a heavy Asian breeze. Pad Thai noodles and red madsamahn curry. Spring rolls with spiced vinaigrette and grilled pork with scallions and red chilies. Carolina was very hungry now, and he looked through the window.

The man looked familiar. Short, with a heavy beard, and wisps of gray hair. He was a performance artist Carolina had seen one night in a club Marie dragged him to, a man who did strange things with finger paints and cucumbers. The man doused himself in the paints, Carolina recalled, then mounted the cucumbers on some sort of waistcoat and danced. The crowd, Marie included, went wild.

Tonight he was dressed in a ragged shirt, jeans, and a pair of worn Birkenstocks. He was pouring wine, and sweating profusely. Then he set the bottle down and raised his glass. Carolina noticed that the glass was sweating as much as the man's soaked forehead. A toast, he appeared to say.

His companion's smile suggested that she appreciated the gesture.

Carolina stepped inside the restaurant. The man noticed him almost immediately and stood up.

"Hello," the little artist said. His companion turned.

"Michael," Marie said, "are you following me?"

Carolina tried to think of something to say. Later he would decide that the response he offered was as good as any other.

"Kinda sleazy, Marie."

Marie Brine flushed, but only for a moment.

"Back off, man," the little artist said. "She made her choice."

Carolina kept his eyes on Marie, but spoke to the artist.

"Why don't you go ask the cook if he has any cucumbers?"

"Could we get a waiter over here?" the artist said, now in a louder voice, that verged on the edge of panic.

"You couldn't tell me, Marie?"

"What was the point?" Marie said, not looking at him. She had transformed herself, from a real person into what he called her "lawyer mode." Argument was useless. She was now an advocate. For herself. Nothing he could say would change her mind.

"We had some fun," Marie said, after a minute. "But you're just too—*normal.*"

"Excuse me?"

"Nothing. Look. We're eating," she said, gesturing at the fuming little artist.

"I'm going to call the waiter," the little artist said.

"What, he didn't hear you the first time?" Carolina turned for the door, which gave the little man more courage.

"Your problem," he said, "is you don't know how to treat a lady."

Carolina said, "I'll keep that in mind if I ever run into one."

He was out the door before Marie or the cucumber artist could respond.

* * *

Narragansett Boulevard was quiet that evening, with almost no traffic in either direction. Carolina drove slowly, gazing idly at the houses, catching glimpses of the water to his left as he rolled back into Edgewood.

Dusk would come in an hour, he thought, judging from the changes in the color of the sky. The blue field was catching strips of pink and red and orange, and lines of purple in between. A sailor's sky, he thought, noticing a pair of boats racing to windward in the channel just beyond Stillhouse Cove.

Carolina had purchased a used Jeep when he decided to stay in Rhode Island, and he pulled it over to the side of the boulevard, parked, and climbed out. The crowds of EMTs and police were long gone. The punctured Boston Whaler had been removed from the yacht club marina piling. A few strands of police line tape were lying in the road, but otherwise there was no sign of the bedlam of a dozen hours before.

Perhaps Marie was right. They were very different people, both with different attitudes about everything. Marie liked modern art and loud clothes. She got a charge out of arguing outrageous positions in court, of representing people accused of horrible crimes.

Carolina tended to keep a lower profile. He dressed well when he had to, when he appeared on television, but what he wore was always conservative. His politics were liberal. But working as a reporter he always felt like a prosecutor.

They had finally come to know one another while he was investigating the death of Lilly Simmons, a producer at Channel Three, and Carolina's onetime lover. Carolina had cared deeply for Lilly, she had such inner strength and integrity. But somehow, they had never quite connected, never found the sort of bond on which to build a lasting relationship. Lilly was pure, sweet, awkward when it came to expressing emotion. Carolina was the same way. They were together, yet separate, enjoying each other but never feeling completely whole. In his most private moments, Carolina always wondered whether he was worthy of her. It was that very doubt that drove him back from Tahiti to Rhode Island, not so much to mourn her as to do something, anything, that would ease his own sense that he had failed to give her what she deserved.

Marie was different. The tall, sleek defense lawyer happened to represent the man wrongfully charged with Lilly's death. The attraction between reporter and lawyer was not immediate, but it was definitely intense. Marie was sultry, sexy, and as fierce as a wolverine. They would thrash in bed as if in combat, clawing and twisting each other's limbs until both wanted to cry out. Making love with Marie was more battle than intimate encounter, an experience that left both of them physically satisfied, but exhausted.

But when Marie's client was cleared and the story was over, Carolina realized, there wasn't much left. She liked to sail, and this was one thing they shared. But sailing, it appeared, wasn't enough.

You're too normal, she had said to him.

What the hell did that mean?

He followed the contours of the cove's edge, looking at the moored boats and the weeds sticking up in the shallows.

Too normal. "Am I too normal?" he asked himself out loud.

A few yards ahead of him he saw a large rock, just off the sidewalk. When he got closer he realized an engraved marker had been welded into the stone.

STILLHOUSE COVE

SITE WHERE LT. WILLIAM DUDINGSTON, COMMANDER OF
THE BRITISH SCHOONER *GASPEE* WAS BROUGHT ASHORE
WOUNDED ON THE NIGHT OF JUNE 10, 1772, AFTER THE
BURNING OF THE *GASPEE*.

There was no one else around, and for a long time Carolina stood and looked out at the cove, wondering what it must have looked like, and what the captain must have felt, landing in this cove, knowing his ship had been lost. The colors in the sky changed again, the red and orange fading to pink and purple.

He looked up at the houses that surrounded the cove. There was a light on in the upstairs turret room of the Queen Anne he'd seen that morning, but the owner was nowhere in sight. The other houses showed no sign of activity. But what struck Carolina were the real estate markers, all of them from a place called Whipple Realty. Of the eight houses he could see, five had SOLD signs in front of them.

He was walking back toward his car when he saw the truck again. It was the same one he had seen that morning, parked by the yacht club marina. Now it was parked just outside the marina gate, the driver's door ajar, the emblem of the Department of Environmental Management just barely visible in the fading light. And that same officer was watching him.

He stopped at his car, and got in. He started the engine, turned the radio on to find a station, then gave up and turned it off again. Carolina reached for the seat belt and realized that the DEM truck had just parked in front of him. The officer climbed out of the cab and walked back to him.

"Evening," she said.

Carolina nodded.

"I couldn't help but notice you."

"Was I doing something wrong?"

"I don't know. Were you?" she asked. Her tone was light.

She stood about five-six, Carolina guessed, perhaps a little more. She had dark brown hair tucked up under a khaki baseball cap, but a few curls poked out here and there. Her face looked tan. On her uniform Carolina saw a small name tag that read TATTAGLIA.

"Not to my knowledge, officer. Just enjoying the view."

"And I thought all you wanted was a story."

Carolina blinked. "I guess you have me at a disadvantage," he said.

"Carla Tattaglia," the woman said, extending a hand.

"You work for DEM?"

"That's right."

He remembered then. She was the officer he'd seen that morning, watching the Cranston police captain debriefing the ATF agents. The lady cop with the sad look on her face.

"What exactly is your beat?" Carolina asked.

"You're looking at it."

She looked out at the cove, now growing black. There was the splash of an unseen fish jumping, then diving back into the weeds and salt water.

"So you're a reporter, aren't you?"

"Yes, for Channel Three."

"I've seen you. Must have been pretty busy today."

"I imagine you were, too."

Officer Tattaglia laughed, but it sounded hollow.

"Did I say something wrong?"

"No," she said. "I just wish what you said was true."

The remark struck Carolina as odd, but he said nothing.

"I'm really just starting my shift," Officer Tattaglia said. "I work a lot of nights. When I was here this morning, I was wrapping up. Only wish I'd been here at the cove an hour earlier."

"What other areas do you cover?"

"Down near Pawtuxet, Greenwich Bay. Sometimes I get to Wickford when we're short on personnel." Tattaglia gave a rueful smile. "Which is most of the time, of course."

"What laws do you enforce?"

"Nearly all the state's coastal pollution regulations. But mostly, I hunt quahoggers."

Nightfall was nearly complete now, and they could see the lights of East Providence winking from across the narrow strip of bay. Farther north, the city of Providence gave off an orange halogen glow on the horizon.

"State's done a lot to clean up the bay," Tattaglia said. "But there's still contamination, especially here in the northern part. It affects the shellfish, but it doesn't kill them. They just keep right on growing."

"And that's a problem?" Carolina asked.

"You bet it is. You get some of these renegade quahoggers in here, they can pull a ton of clams out of these shallow beds. Make a thousand dollars on a good night, selling to some distributor who resells down in New York. Then someone orders up cherrystones or a bowl of chowder in a seafood restaurant and goes home with a dose of hepatitis."

"Really?" Carolina leaned forward. "What kind of penalties does the state have?"

"They're tough. If they're caught with an illegal load, we can seize it, and seize the boat. Then there are fines. Sometimes we can even throw the quahoggers in jail. But first you have to catch them."

"And I imagine," Carolina said, "that's pretty hard to do when you have just one officer covering twenty miles of coastline."

Officer Tattaglia wore her rueful smile once again. She looked as though she were about to reply when her head snapped around.

The noise was faint, but constant. The sound of boat engines. Carolina could not tell which direction it came from.

"Is that—" Carolina stopped when he saw Tattaglia raise a finger to her lips.

Gradually, the sound grew stronger. Carla Tattaglia remained absolutely still, her eyes locked on the water. Carolina did the same. The engines seemed to be at low throttle, just enough to keep from stalling. Every now and then the operator would goose the power a little, then quickly slow down again.

After about three minutes, Carla Tattaglia pointed. Carolina followed, but saw nothing. Then, just outside the cover, there was a flicker as the craft passed in front of some lights in East Providence, briefly cutting them off.

All Carolina could see was a boat, a skiff, pushed by the quiet engines. There was someone near the stern, but the person was nothing more than a human shape.

Carla dropped her hand. She still made no sound, and Carolina wondered for a moment whether she was holding her breath.

The skiff drew closer. The boat driver had ceased use of the throttle altogether, and the little craft seemed to be coasting. Finally, in the dimness, Carolina was able to make out the shape of a man, a short man, driving the boat. Despite his small size, he looked powerful, and the low light revealed long, bushy hair. The skiff he drove made a long, slow circle inside the cove.

"Hello, Mitty," Carla Tattaglia murmured. "Got any clams?"

The man she called Mitty continued to glide, oblivious, cutting only a slight, near colorless wake behind him.

From the yacht club, Carolina heard the sound of a car starting. Carla Tattaglia cringed, but remained still. The man in the skiff heard the noise, too. In a moment his engines started up again. The car's lights came on, shooting a beam across the cove. For a moment the skiff was caught in it, and in that instant Carolina and Tattaglia both saw the boat was empty, save for Mitty, a large bull rake and a few canvas bags. Then the skiff throttled up, and shot back out of the cove. The car from the yacht club backed up, turned, and pulled out of the lot. In a few minutes the sound of the boat's engines faded. Carolina could tell the skiff was headed south, to be lost soon in the wider expanses of Narragansett Bay.

Carla Tattaglia was quiet, but Carolina could tell she was angry.

"That one of the guys you want to bust?"

Tattaglia nodded.

"Seemed to spook pretty easily."

"I suppose," she said. "These guys aren't that smart, you know? If they were, they'd find another way to make a living where they wouldn't risk losing their livelihood every time they go to work. But they're shrewd. Real shrewd."

"You ever seen that fellow before?"

"Lots of times," Carla Tattaglia said.

"Why do I get the feeling," Carolina said, "that you're not just looking at him for illegal shellfishing?"

Carla said nothing. But she smiled again, and this time it was not rueful. Carolina decided he liked that smile.

"Do you think these quahoggers had something to do with the explosion this morning?"

The smile faded.

"I've got to get to work," Tattaglia said. "It's after ten o'clock."

"Do you think I could ride with you some evening?" Carolina asked. "Might make an interesting story. Maybe even get your department some more money for extra officers."

"You'd have to talk to my supervisor," Carla said. "But it's fine with me."

She began to walk back toward her truck.

"Officer," Carolina said. Tattaglia turned.

"You've been very helpful. I think DEM is lucky to have you."

Carolina couldn't see her face as she was driving away, but he hoped she was smiling again.

Ocean State Hospital had returned to its usual routine. The night-shift nurses were making rounds, checking paperwork at the central desk, or chatting quietly with one another in the corridors. The staff physicians were gone for the day, and the orderlies were down in emergency, trying to assist with the usual spate of patients: victims of drunk driving accidents, participants in bar fights, the occasional shooting victim. There was almost no indication that earlier in the day the famed medical institution had been infiltrated by renegade members of the press.

Almost. On the fifth floor, a special hospital security guard had been posted outside one ward. He was under orders to check the credentials of anyone seeking to enter the room. Only nurses, doctors, or police officers under escort were to be allowed inside.

The security guard in question, however, had a serious concern that Ocean State's medical staff had failed to take into consideration: he desperately needed to go to the bathroom. This was a frequent problem for this particular guard, since he habitually consumed at least a quart of beer before reporting for the eleven to seven shift. A visit to the rest room in the first hour of his shift usually remedied his bladder discomfort. But tonight, the orders were that he could not leave his post. Such an order was proving to be intolerable.

Unfortunately for the guard, a nurse was making it difficult for him to slip away. She seemed to be checking every ward room on the wing, and doing an exceptionally slow job of it. Each room appeared to take about three minutes, but the guard could never be sure. The nurse seemed to work at a leisurely pace. Still, the guard was catching a pattern. Yes, he was sure it was taking the nurse about three minutes each time she visited a new room. If he waited until she disappeared into a room, he should have enough time to take care of business.

At precisely 11:54 P.M., the nurse emerged from a ward room two doors away. She took her time moving down the hall, apparently checking charts posted outside the door. She moved closer, looking at the charts on the door of the room next door. The guard squirmed, jamming his legs together, trying to think of something dry while at the same time willing the nurse to enter the adjacent room. Finally, at 11:54:30, the nurse entered the other room.

The guard bolted for the toilet located inside the ward. He left the door to the room ajar, in case the nurse appeared, but closed the door to the bathroom.

At precisely 11:54:45, the nurse entered the room. She listened briefly at the door to the bathroom. Upon hearing the unique sound of water hitting water, she moved quickly to the only bed occupied by a patient. The man's head remained heavily bandaged. He was asleep.

From her pocket the nurse withdrew a small syringe. There was nothing in the syringe, but this was not necessary. She took hold of the man's left arm and expertly felt until she spotted a vein that would support a needle's entry. The nurse pulled the plunger back with one hand and inserted the needle into the man's arm. Then she swiftly punched the syringe plunger down, hard, driving a small pocket of air into the man's veins. She removed the needle, capped it, and replaced it in her pocket.

Almost immediately, the sleeping patient convulsed. As this began, the toilet flushed. At 11:55:24, the security guard emerged from the bathroom and noticed the jerky motions of the patient. A small machine hooked up next to the man's IV emitted a high-pitched chirping noise that quickly turned into a steady beep.

The guard wondered briefly if the machine was specially wired to sound an alarm whenever someone failed to wash their hands after flushing the toilet. He had heard of similar devices being employed in restaurant men's rooms. Such was not the case, however.

Within a minute, another nurse, this one a male, appeared in the room. Checking the patient's pulse, the male nurse quietly swore an oath and pushed the security guard out of the way so he could reach a button and call a code. As an ER doctor arrived and orderlies wheeled in a crash cart, the security guard wondered what happened to the nurse he'd seen checking the other patients' rooms.

He was too shocked, however, and too worried about his own job to say anything to anyone. Later, the guard would decide it was best to say nothing about the nurse, since by doing so he would have to admit he had left his post to take a leak.

As the code team gathered on the fifth floor of Ocean State Hospital, a woman dressed as a nurse walked out the emergency entrance. She walked calmly and quickly toward her car, lighting a cigarette. She took a deep drag and exhaled through her nose, absently clutching at her shoulders. Despite the warmth of the summer evening, she still felt very cold.

6

The rain that fell in early morning beat the windows and roof of Carolina's apartment like a thousand people clapping. It stopped just before Carolina woke, and when he looked outside, he thought he saw steam coming off the glistening pavement. The day would require light clothes.

Shirley was talking with the assignment editor, a slender young man with acne and a mustache that desperately needed to be shaved. Carolina nodded good morning. The assignment editor looked nervous. Shirley looked pained.

"What's up?"

"Your buddy the dynamited diver," Shirley said.

"What about him?"

"He's dead."

Carolina looked at Shirley, the editor, and back again.

"It happened too late for the paper," the editor said. "But I caught it making beat calls when I came in. Cranston cops told me they were sending someone to the hospital."

"When was that?" Carolina asked.

"About two hours ago," the editor replied, wincing.

"Before you go beating on Billy for not calling you," Shirley said, "I want you to know that we're on this. We have a crew at the hospital."

"You getting anywhere?"

"Your performance yesterday hasn't exactly made it easier for us. I've got a call in to Bleeder, but he hasn't returned it."

"Why don't I go over there?" Carolina asked.

"Why don't I throw a match in a bucket of gasoline?" Shirley looked aggravated. "Jesus, Michael, whatever happened to the guy, is it worth burning bridges with the major health institution in the state? One of our anchors does a health-watch report over there each week."

"One of those bullshit PR segments where they get to talk about how great they are?"

They were in Shirley's office now. She reached instinctively for a bottle of vitamins, then popped one and washed it down with a slug of coffee. Shirley cringed in disgust.

"Cold. I hate cold coffee."

Carolina suppressed a smile.

"Michael, what you just referred to as bullshit other people call a community service. When the hell did you turn into such a cynic?"

The monitors of the three network affiliates were carrying daytime talk shows. After a moment, Carolina realized that all three shows carried satellite interviews with the same guest: a cross-dresser on death row in a Southern prison. He was trying to explain why he thought he should be permitted a marriage license so that he could exchange vows with another convict. With the volume turned down the convict's explanation was lost but cutaways showed the audience members intermittently crying, jeering, and applauding.

"I don't know," Carolina said. "Perhaps I'm just a victim of the times in which I live."

Shirley smiled. "You are such a ballbuster."

"Yeah."

"Listen," she said, "there's a lot of other stories to work on today. I'd like to get you started on a series about casino gambling."

"Shirley."

"Really. It has a lot of potential. We could send you—"

"Shirley."

"What?"

"Did they move the body? The diver's body?"

"Yes. We had pictures at seven twenty-five."

"Let me have an hour."

"I don't want you going over to that hospital."

"I won't go over there."

"Rhode Island Medical Examiner."

"Arthur Goulet please."

"Who may I say is calling?"

"This is Phipps over at Ocean State Pathology. We've got some test results, and I was told to call."

"I'm sorry, he's tied up right now."

"I was told that this is urgent."

"Hold, please."

Carolina looked at his watch. He wondered how long Goulet had been up. After a minute, a hoarse voice came on the line.

"Goulet."

"How's it going, Arthur?"

"Caro—uh, yes, what can I do for you?"

"Been a while, hasn't it?"

"I see. And what about the blood work?"

"I need some information, Arthur."

"I'll need to write that down, and it's a little noisy in here. Let me put you on hold."

Carolina waited another ten seconds.

"I can't believe you called me here," Goulet said when he came back on the line.

"Where else was I going to reach you?"

"The new ME started last week. He was standing right next to me."

"Were you working on that diver from Ocean State Hospital?"

"Yeah. I figured that's why you're calling."

"What's his name?"

"I don't know. Come on, Mike, I can get in a lot of trouble. I've only been back from my suspension a couple of months."

"No you won't. Besides, who helped you get your job back?"

"Who got me suspended in the first place?"

"That wasn't me, Arthur, it was your former boss."

"Yeah, well, if you hadn't pushed me to help you on that story about him moonlighting, I never woulda been suspended."

"If you hadn't been collecting old body parts in your refrigerator, Stupfeld wouldn't have been able to discredit you."

"Hey, them parts weren't worth nothing. I'm no thief, you said so yourself."

"That's true. Look, Arthur, I'm not trying to relive old times. I need your help. They're freezing me out over at Ocean State."

"I know. ATF's here, talking about the stunt you pulled."

"Then you know what happened. Are you going to help me?"

Goulet was quiet for a moment.

Finally, he said, "ATF's rolling the guy's fingerprints right now."

"I know his first name is Anthony," Carolina said. "If they hit something, will they call you?"

"That's what the agent said. Probably take a couple hours."

"And?"

"And—if I get the last name, I'll drop you a dime."

"Is ATF pretty sure they'll match up a print?"

"Yeah."

"Why?"

"Two reasons. First, the guy's got needle tracks up his arm, so he could have a criminal record."

"What's the other?"

"His tattoo."

"What tattoo?"

"The one on his upper arm with the anchor and the flag. I think the guy was in the navy."

Carolina spent the next two hours reading clippings from the Providence *Herald* about the progress of gambling legislation in the Rhode Island General Assembly.

The primary push for a referendum, he noticed, came from a couple of Native American tribes in southern Rhode Island.

Their interest in a casino, he noticed, had risen in direct proportion to the success of another Indian casino in southeastern Connecticut. The Rhode Island tribes had hired lobbyists and public relations people to advance their cause. The result was a massive campaign on radio and television, stressing the economic benefits of legalized gambling. There was also a grassroots effort that included rallies like the one held in the State House the day before.

Just before noon, Carolina walked back into his boss's office. Shirley was eating a cup of yogurt. She paused between bites to drag on a cigarette.

"I was wondering."

Shirley looked at him and wolfed some yogurt.

"The Indians are supposed to be pushing this gambling referendum, right?"

"Right."

"And the idea is that they will control the casino and share revenue with the state?"

"Yes," Shirley said, inhaling. "So?"

"So how come this referendum isn't limited to the question of Indian gaming?"

Shirley gave him a blank look.

"What I mean," Carolina said, "is the referendum asks whether a casino can be licensed *anywhere* in Rhode Island, subject to state licensing and approval."

"The tribes are the only ones who've been interested," Shirley said. Her tone was cautious, as if she were testing the validity of her own words.

"They're the only ones you've heard about," Carolina said. Before he could say more the overhead speaker paged him to a telephone. Shirley picked up her handset and offered it to him.

"I was right," Arthur Goulet said. "Military guys always have prints."

"Who is it?"

"Name's Anthony Palumbo. From Westerly."

"What else?"

"I just work here, Mike. They don't tell me much."

"Don't bullshit me, Arthur. You hang around that cutting room. I know you heard something else."

Goulet waited again. When he spoke his voice was low.

"If this comes back at me I'm in serious trouble."

"You know I won't do that," Carolina said.

"Okay. They think the guy once went through Navy SEAL training. That's where ATF thinks he learned how to dive. But then something went wrong, and he washed out."

"So what was he doing in the cove?"

"That's the weird part. No one seems to know."

"Well, what does he do for a living? He run a dive shop or something?"

"No."

"Then what?"

"He's a croupier."

"Excuse me?"

"A crew-pee-yay, you know? He tends crap games at that casino in Connecticut. Or blackjack. Something like that."

"What's the cause and manner?"

"ME thinks it's an air bubble to the heart. It's homicide, Michael. Definitely homicide."

Confirming Goulet's information proved difficult. Carolina started with ATF.

"Where did you get this," Bert Schumacher wanted to know.

"A little bird told me," Carolina said.

"Call our office in Boston," Bert Schumacher told him. "I'm not supposed to talk to the press."

"After all the fun we had together yesterday?" Carolina asked.

"That was a onetime thing."

"It's going to become public anyway."

"Only when our investigation is complete," Schumacher said.

"Did this guy work in the SEALs?"

"You know," Schumacher said, "you really are aggravating."

"It's part of my charm," Carolina said.

"All right. I'm only going to say this once, and then you're going to back off so I can do my job." Schumacher gave Carolina a number in Washington to call.

The number was for a public affairs office at the Pentagon. After dropping the ATF's name, Carolina learned that Anthony Palumbo, DOB 3/24/61, of Westerly, Rhode Island, received a general discharge from the United States Navy in 1988. The office had no information regarding Palumbo's duties or where he was stationed. Shirley tapped him on the shoulder as he hung up the phone.

"There's a press conference in half an hour down at Stillhouse Cove."

"Who called it?"

"One of the preservation groups. Has something to do with the explosion."

The skies were clear, but the air was still wet and heavy as a blanket. The afternoon sun had pushed temperatures into the low nineties, unusually high for Rhode Island in June.

The gathering outside the Rhode Island Yacht Club parking lot was much smaller than the day before. There were no police, no rescue vehicles, and no curious onlookers trying to figure out what was happening. The photographers from the three network stations were all perspiring as they set up their equipment. A young radio reporter, barely out of college, fumbled with a package of batteries he was trying to insert in a tape recorder.

There was a slight breeze coming off the northern bay, and this inhibited the woman strutting about, handing out copies of a press release typed on brown, recycled paper. A small gust almost carried the pages away, but the woman crushed and trapped most of them against her chest, then stomped on a few more with a thick rope-soled sandal. She handed a wrinkled page to Carolina.

The boards of Ocean State Preservation and Save the Chowder today announce a joint agreement seeking to declare Stillhouse Cove off-limits to all commercial and recreational boaters.

A need for this restriction exists until the impact of yesterday's explosion can be assessed. Serious questions still exist as to whether that explosion has stirred the remains of the British naval cutter *Gaspee.* If in fact artifacts from this vessel have been found, then it is vital that every piece be properly documented and preserved.

Similarly, Save the Chowder believes that the explosion may have harmed the local shellfish population. While commercial harvesting of cherrystones and quahogs is prohibited in this area, Save the Chowder believes additional funding for existing restrictions will better protect the environment and our state's history.

The paper seemed to wilt slightly in the humidity. Carolina folded and tucked it into a back pocket. He walked over to Earl.

"Save the Chowder?"

"Sure," Earl said with a smile. "But leave me a bowl."

A man in his fifties, wearing a bow tie and tweed jacket, stepped up to the small bank of microphones that the photographers had assembled on a lighting stand. The man's face was slightly pinched, and it turned red as he cleared his throat.

"Good afternoon. My name is Garrison Pinker, and I'm chairman of the Ocean State Preservation Society."

Pinker spoke for about two minutes, essentially repeating the statements contained in the sodden press release. He sounded earnest, but somewhat tired, Carolina thought, as he sought public support for his cause.

A moment later the woman shod in sandals stepped up to the microphones.

"We're here today not just to save a ship, but to—"

"Say your name and spell it," one of the TV reporters interrupted.

"Uh, Sally. Sally Generous, and I'm here on behalf of Save the Chowder. As I said, we are also here today to save the public and Narragansett Bay's shellfish population from environmental disaster. What happened here yesterday should serve as a warning that our bay is in danger. That diver had no business in the waters of this pristine cove. It certainly looks like his actions are behind the explosion. . . ."

Carolina could notice several reporters scribbling down that last remark, while a few others stopped writing and shook their heads. Sally spoke for another five minutes, advocating for a complete ban on diving, boating, or fishing in the bay. The reporters listened quietly, though a couple of yachtsmen from the club thumbed their noses as they drove past into the club. Evidently they had seen Sally before.

When Generous finished, Pinker offered to take questions.

"What makes you think that the wood taken after the explosion yesterday belongs to the *Gaspee?*" the radio reporter asked.

"We are seeking," Pinker said, swallowing, "to have the wood tested by one of the academic departments at Brown or the University of Rhode Island."

A television reporter asked, "Do you know anything about the investigation into the explosion?" Both Pinker and Generous shook their heads.

"Then do you have any evidence," Carolina asked, "that the explosion is somehow related to clam digging?"

Pinker said nothing. Sally Generous looked down, carefully examining some pebbles at the toe of her sandal.

"It's common knowledge," she said finally, "that certain qua-hoggers have been illegally fishing the northern part of the bay for years."

"Sounds like you're speculating," Carolina said.

Generous's face flashed with anger. She didn't like being questioned.

"I just know," she said. The reporters chuckled.

The press conference broke up. Sally Generous headed straight for Carolina.

"You just don't understand," she said.

"Yes I do," Carolina said. "Yesterday, there was an accident here. No one knows yet how it happened or why. But today, you want to use that accident to suit your own cause."

Sally Generous looked momentarily deflated.

"Does that mean we won't get a sound bite tonight?"

"I don't know," Carolina said.

"I know I'm right."

"Maybe you are. But you don't have much to prove it."

Sally Generous sniffed. "Isn't it your job to investigate?"

Carolina smiled. "Yes it is. And if you wouldn't waste my time, maybe I could."

"Your piece seems a little thin, tonight," Shirley Templeton observed.

"I'm inclined to agree," Carolina said. He kept his eyes on the monitors, not looking at her.

"I guess those people at the press conference didn't have a lot to offer."

"I guess not."

"Getting Palumbo's name was good."

"Yes."

"Other stations didn't have that."

"No."

"I'm not sure this story has legs."

"Sure it does," Carolina said.

"I'd rather have you working on the gambling series."

"That reminds me."

"What?"

"How many stories have we done about ex-casino employees who are hospitalized after mysterious explosions who suddenly wind up dead?"

"We haven't confirmed that he worked in the casino."

"If I didn't have to go to that press conference we would have."

Shirley, momentarily stung, remained silent for a moment. Then she said, "You know we had to cover that. We're television. We need fresh pictures whenever we can get them."

"I know that," Carolina said. "Have you considered the possibility there might be a connection between Palumbo and the gambling story?"

"I have," Shirley said, her voice flat. "I'm just not sure I can wait until the millennium for you to find it."

Now Carolina looked stung.

"If I were to let you stay on this thing," Shirley said, "what would you do next?"

Carolina thought for a moment. Sally Generous of Save the Chowder may not have had any evidence, but her accusations served as a reminder.

"I wonder if you'd mind," he said, "letting me work late?"

iesel fuel has a distinctive smell, even more so when mixed with salt air. It is a hard odor that seems to bite and hold, numbing the other senses like some kind of strange workman's narcotic. Carolina liked the smell. It reminded him of marinas in the Caribbean and the South Seas, of old boats and new harbors, and the people he had met in all of those places.

"What makes you so happy?" Carla Tattaglia asked. She removed the nozzle from the tank and replaced it on the dockside pump. "Aren't you working late?"

"Sure," Carolina said. "But it's still nice to get back on the water."

Nightfall brought a slight change in climate. The air was still warm, but the humidity eased. There was still some breeze, but it no longer felt stifling, the way it had earlier at the press conference on the edge of Stillhouse Cove. The murky water of the marina shimmered, reflecting splashes of orange halogen light.

"Mind casting off that line?"

Carolina slipped the springline that helped to hold the police boat to the dock. He neatly coiled and stowed it near a cleat on the bow.

"You seem to know what you're doing," Tattaglia said.

She was dressed in khaki again, along with a cap and deck shoes. She might have been a deckhand, maybe even a ship's officer on a commercial vessel, Carolina thought, except for the .38 revolver strapped to her side. Carolina wore jeans and a short-sleeved crew shirt. In a small gym bag he'd brought along a hand-held "Hi-8" millimeter camera. There were no extra photographers available.

"Do you people always give such short notice?" Tattaglia asked.

"Most of the time," Carolina said.

"I can't guarantee you're going to see anything."

"I didn't expect that you would."

"Just so we understand each other."

The police boat was clearing the marina now, the engine running nicely as they slipped into Greenwich Bay. In fifteen minutes they were past the light on Warwick Neck and heading north. The shoreline on both sides came closer as the bay narrowed.

"Not as much room to maneuver up here," Carolina said.

"No," Tattaglia said, not looking at him.

"Does that help you?"

"It can. Then again, it can work against you, too."

Carla cut the engine. The tide was in full flood, and she let the boat ride with it. She said nothing, listening for the sound of other boats.

In the next half hour they saw a large power yacht coming south from Providence, engines full speed. A sailboat, motoring toward one of the yacht clubs. But no clam skiffs could be seen. Carolina began to relax.

"So what do you know about the *Gaspee?*" he asked quietly.

"What do you want to know?"

"Everything."

Tattaglia lifted her cap from her head, smoothed her hair, and replaced it again. "Let's see," she said. "The story goes back to the 1770s, when the British were taxing everything that moved, either in or out of the colonies. The British navy was used to keep traders and merchants from moving goods without first paying duty to the crown.

"So Rhode Islanders started smuggling. They'd run small vessels up the bay, usually at night, and the British had a hard time catching them. The *Gaspee* was one of the ships assigned to patrol Narragansett Bay.

"One night, she caught sight of a smuggler, and she chased it. The *Gaspee* was faster than the smaller boat, but the captain of the smuggler knew the waters better. He took his boat right up here, where we are, then in toward shore near a place called Pawtuxet Cove. The *Gaspee* was right behind him.

"But the smaller boat had a shallow draft. And the *Gaspee*'s captain and crew were so anxious to catch the smuggler they didn't pay much attention. The *Gaspee* ran aground. The smugglers were beside themselves, because no one had ever trapped a British ship like this before. Somebody found a horse, I guess, and rode to Providence to ask the merchants what to do."

"And word came back to burn it?"

"To the waterline," Carla said.

"And this is a true story?"

"Certainly," Carla said, mildly offended.

"Quite a story," Carolina said. "Kind of like the Boston Tea Party."

"It happened five months before the Boston Tea Party, and nobody paraded around pretending to be an Indian, either. In fact, one of the smugglers later became a captain in the Continental Navy."

"Really?"

Carla nodded. "Abraham Whipple. A few years later he engaged a British ship, and the English commander recognized him. Said he was going to hang him from the yardarm."

"And?"

"Whipple said, 'Always catch a man before you hang him.' As far as I know he got away."

"How does a police officer know so much about colonial history?"

"What, youse t'ink I should be sittin' home drinkin' bee-ah and watchin' 'Cops' on TV?"

The affected Rhode Island accent caught Carolina by surprise and made him laugh. Carla smiled.

"Brown University," she said when he stopped. "Bachelor's degree in American history."

"No shit."

"No shit."

Two hours went by.

They had heard engines twice more, but seen nothing. Tattaglia moved the boat once more, closer to the entrance of Stillhouse Cove. But without actually seeing anything, there was little to do.

Carolina was tired, and found it hard to keep his eyes open. "I think maybe this is a write-off," he said.

"Maybe," Tattaglia said.

Had they not stopped talking just then, they might have missed it. But both of them caught the soft sound of a motor at extreme low throttle. Carolina recognized it. The same sound as the engine he'd heard from the shoreline the night before.

"Then again, maybe not," Tattaglia murmured.

The bucket held about five rakeloads of clams. They were oozing slime, spitting seawater, and shifting in the bucket when the boat rocked.

Mitt Navel chewed quietly on a piece of his beard. He always did that when he was feeling stress. One bucket wouldn't buy a load of gas or a pitcher of beer. But that was all he had found.

On a good night he could fill the skiff with quahogs, high enough he'd have to wade through them to tie up. He could sell them to a restaurant, or one of the wholesalers from out of town, maybe clear a thousand, then go home and sleep until the sun was going down. He hadn't done that in more than a week, hadn't raked any clams for three days, and then it was eight hours in the sun with a bunch of stiffs, raking legal in broad daylight. He humped and dumped for eight hours straight and barely cleared two hundred.

There was a high-pitched sound in the darkness. A clam squeal, he liked to call it, as a mollusk pinched water through a snout. Sometimes he wondered if they were talking to him, trying to tell him where he could find more.

But that was not the only distraction. There were boat engines that came and went, the noises fading and then reappearing whenever his guard went down.

The radio said that the diver was dead. Well, too fucking bad. All Mitt had wanted to do was scare him a little, just keep him away from the cove. What the hell was he doing there, anyway?

There was that sound again. A boat engine. Goose the throttle and fade, goose and fade, the way he'd done it the night before when he came to check out the cove again. Someone trying to be quiet.

A clam squealed again. Mitty was nervous. It just wasn't a good night. He needed to get home, sit down, maybe watch some cable. Another couple days, he could come back and it would be okay. He picked up the oars, slipped them into their locks, and started hauling. When he got clear of the cove he could fire up and motor down to Pawtuxet.

The roar seemed to come from nowhere, a monstrous, wrenching sound, a gasoline-powered belch. Mitty looked around, but saw nothing. Instinctively, he yanked the oars in and went for his own engine. But before he could get there the big thing emerged from the dark, and the eruption of sound died as quickly as it came.

As it glided toward him a spotlight flared and caught Mitty looking like a deer. There was someone on the bow, leaning forward. He reached out with a boat hook and expertly caught hold of the painter on the front of Mitty's clam skiff.

"Hey, fuckface," a voice said. "Jimmy Flannery wants to talk to you."

* * *

"That's a cigarette," Carolina said. "Only boat I know that makes a sound as ugly as that."

"Do you see it?" Carla asked.

For a moment he did not. The noise rumbled across the water, then floated away.

Then he saw the light, sweeping the water and settling on a small boat, painted gray. There was a man caught in the light, but it was impossible to make out any features.

"Over there," Carolina said.

"I see it," Carla said, kicking over her engine. The police boat jerked once and then reared up. As it gained speed Tattaglia made a graceful turn and threw on her siren.

The other boats were at least a half mile away. In less than ten seconds the police boat was at full throttle, Tattaglia at the console, Carolina hanging on to a gunwale for dear life.

Carla threw on a spotlight of her own. She steered with one hand, and trained the light with the other. Just before the boats came into view, the distinctive sound of gunshots punched through the noise of the engines.

The smaller boat was a clam skiff. The larger one was indeed a cigarette, long and sleek, made of hot purple fiberglass. A lightning bolt hung the length of the boat's port side. Beneath the shock of jagged yellow color were a matching set of yellow letters that bore the boat's name, but Carolina was too far away to make the letters out.

Carla Tattaglia grabbed a microphone that fed into a loudspeaker on the police boat's console.

"Clam skiff and cigarette boat. Clam skiff and cigarette boat. This is Rhode Island DEM. Cut your engines and prepare to be boarded. I repeat, cut your engines and prepare to be boarded."

The cigarette did not respond. But within seconds, it roared again and took off down the bay. Carla was on the radio, calling for backup.

"What can I do?" Carolina said.

"Keep the light on the clam boat," Carla responded. Carolina grabbed the spot, but when the light found the skiff again it was empty, no one aboard. The clam digger had apparently gone over the side.

"Shit," Carla muttered. She turned the boat again, going after the cigarette, the awful sound of the big boat drowning everything else.

The police boat was fast, capable of better than fifty knots. But the cigarette was faster. They chased for the better part of five minutes, running full speed down the bay, until they were close to Patience Island. Gradually, the sound of the cigarette began to fade, until it was little more than a distant roar.

Carla muttered quietly, then swung the boat in a gentle arc. They headed back toward Providence.

"What the hell was that all about?" Carolina asked.

Tattaglia bit her lip. She did not look at him.

They passed Pawtuxet Cove in another five minutes. Carla lowered the throttle and turned the spot on again. She swung the boat over and over the western shoreline, all the way up to Rhode Island Yacht Club and back again.

The inky brine turned gold and silver in the light's reflection. But the skiff had slipped away like some ghostly smuggler running from British guns.

The cigarette boat was just over thirty-five feet, bow to engine exhaust. Her hull was indeed purple, and lightning bolts ran the length of the port and starboard sides. Beneath these wicked yellow slash marks were two words: BREAKING WIND.

Jimmy Flannery knew people laughed when they saw his boat. He didn't care. Jimmy didn't care about much of anything except taking care of his business and having a few laughs when time permitted. Besides, it wasn't registered in his name.

The boat was for pleasure, like being seen when he wanted to be seen, or entertaining the odd bimbo. When he wasn't around it could be used for a fast run offshore to a larger boat waiting to off-load a little product, though he kept such transactions to a minimum. Either way, he liked the name. Fuck anyone who couldn't take the joke.

But this morning was not a time for joking. The fishing piers of Point Judith were still quiet when the cigarette pulled in, but within an hour it would be crawling with men going to work. Jimmy did not want to be around then.

He stood with his arms crossed as two men tied his boat to the cleats. There were signs everywhere saying that the pier was for commercial fishing vessels only, but no one ever bothered Flannery's boat. The crewmen took their time making sure the lines were secure, almost as if they were trying to delay any confrontation.

"There ain't no fuckin' hurricane comin'," Jimmy said when he finally lost patience. "You get what I wanted or not?"

"Had a lil' problem, Jimmy," one of the men said, shaking his head.

"What kind of problem?"

"Some kind of cop showed up."

"Who? State police? Feds?"

"Nah, Environmental."

"What?"

Jimmy Flannery stood, lips pursed, while his two soldiers explained. He was less than six feet tall, but gave the impression of being much taller. The shock of hair he wore in a neat part was practically snow white. As he listened, his face grew more and more florid.

"So youse didn't get nothin'?"

The two soldiers winced.

"Well?"

"No, Jimmy," the second one said. "The fuckin' cops."

"Fuckin' cops," Jimmy sneered. "Some Environmental officer. Pussy police. I want to know why that sawed-off little clamdigger was muckin' around."

"We know you do, Jimmy, we know," the first one said.

"I've got a lot at stake."

The men nodded.

"And if you can't get this done for me, then I'll find someone who can."

"We'll keep trying, Jimmy," the second one said.

"You put out the word?"

"All over, just like you told us," the first one said.

"Good. I want to know what that clamdigger knows."

"Right, boss."

"Then I want you to help him take a nap with his clams."

8

In Warwick and East Greenwich, at the fish wholesalers and the restaurants and the waterfront dives, the word spread fast. Mitty Navel found this out when he tried to unload his two buckets of clams.

"Gedda fug oudda heeea," said a grizzled man who ran a fish shop called Carmine's Seafood DEE-lights.

" 'S good clams, Carmine," Mitty said, holding up a bucket of oozing shells.

"Don't need 'em, don't want 'em. Probably give my customers the clap."

"Can't get that from clams," Mitty said.

But Carmine wasn't listening. He was too busy dumping a mess of fish heads into the trash.

Mitty had even less luck at Persico's Shellfish, which brokered quahogs to restaurants in New York. The man saw him coming and locked the door.

"You never done this before," Mitty cried, pounding on the glass.

"Youse never been a dead man before," the man called from inside.

"Whadda youse mean?" Mitty said.

"Ask Jimmy Flannery."

Mitty climbed into his truck, an old gray Toyota held together by bondo and rust. He drove to a tavern down by the edge of Greenwich Cove called Maria's. Maria's was run by a retired sanitation worker named Salvatore Migliori, who had christened the bar after his dead wife.

All of Salvatore's customers called him Ashcan, a tribute to the clump of gray hair on his head. His tavern was a hangout for quahoggers, including those who humped and dumped by the light of the moon. There were two customers in the bar when Mitty walked in just after ten A.M. Both immediately broke for the back door.

"You're killin' my business," Ashcan wailed.

"Wanna buy some clams?" Mitty said hopefully, holding up a bucket.

"Not a chance."

"Good fuggin' clams."

"No way, Mitty. No fuckin' way."

Mitty sat down, dejected. He set his bucket on the floor. One of the clams squirted brine across the leg of his jeans. Mitty checked his pockets and came up with four single dollar bills, three dimes, a nickel, and a penny.

"I'm thirsty," he said.

Sal drew a cheap draft into a dirty eight-ounce glass. He set the beer in front of Mitty, then wiped his hands on an apron that might once have been white.

"Buck twenty-five."

Mitty gave him two dollars. "Ashcan."

"What?" Sal was still upset over losing two customers and gaining only one.

"Who's Jimmy Flannery?"

Sal almost choked as he counted out three quarters.

"Mitty," he said, in a voice that almost sounded concerned. "What the fuck did you do?"

Mitt Navel swallowed half the beer before he answered. When he set the glass down a small line of foam had appeared on the facial hair that rimmed his mouth.

"I didn't do nothin'."

Sal looked at his customer, his grimy hand wrapped around the glass, two buckets of dirty clams oozing and hissing at his feet. Sal almost felt sorry for him.

"Youse done somethin', and you better figure out what."

Mitty Navel did not look up. He just stood and grabbed his clams before heading for the tavern door.

"Hey," Sal called after him, "what about my tip?"

"You look like you didn't get much sleep," Shirley said.

"Thanks," Carolina replied, "you look great, too."

"How did your little expedition go?"

"My curiosity is piqued," he said, and told her what happened.

"Did you get the name of the boat?" Shirley asked when he was through. Carolina shook his head.

"I'll tell you, though, I'd recognize that boat again. Just like one of the waterborne pimp machines you used to see on 'Miami Vice'."

"Well," Shirley said, "maybe you'll get the chance. In the meantime, we need a story."

"I want to find out more about who this dead diver is."

"That's wonderful," Shirley said. "Can you get me something by six?"

Carolina ignored the question. "Do you think you could spare Earl? And we're going to need that new hidden camera rig you bought."

Shirley crossed her arms. "I'm still waiting to hear whether you can get something by six."

Carolina said nothing.

"Look," Shirley said, "I know you want to investigate. But we need a story. I've got—"

"I know, I know, the general manager is on your ass. Money is tight. We're short-staffed."

Shirley smiled.

"It would be nice," Carolina said, "if we could add something new to this dialogue."

"I recognize your frustration," Shirley said.

"Sure, but you're not going to do anything about it. No one is. That's the problem with this business. It's always the bottom line. What have you done lately? All those other stupid clichés."

"That's the game," Shirley said. "Every night people turn on the tube and they want to know what's going on. It's a big hungry monster, and it has to be fed every day."

"Yeah," Carolina said, "but we usually serve junk food."

Shirley flinched. Carolina held his ground. It was an uncomfortable moment, each one knowing the other was right, but neither one willing to give in.

"I guess," Shirley said finally, "I could spare you for a while."

"Thank you."

"Will you at least try to get something for tonight?"

"I always try."

"I'd feel better," Shirley said, "if you'd always try a little harder."

Carolina smiled. "I promise."

"Mind telling me where you're going?"

"Looking for a game."

For years, the biggest employer in southern Rhode Island and eastern Connecticut was Electric Boat. In factories and shops along the Thames River, thousands of men and women went to work each day to draft and cut, to weld and rivet the materials that would form Los Angeles class and Trident submarines. Many of the ships were later berthed just up the river at the naval base in Groton. The others disappeared into the mist and water, only to surface later in Holyloch, Scotland, Kings Bay, Georgia, or Bangor, Washington.

But the collapse of the Cold War meant a restructuring for Electric Boat. There were fewer and fewer jobs as the demand for submarines eased.

Into the economic void stepped an obscure tribe of Native Americans, armed with a federal court decision guaranteeing their sovereignty over tribal lands. The tribal members, few in number, were interested in preserving their heritage. But they were even more interested in making bucks. Big bucks.

Deep in the woods, perhaps fifteen or twenty miles from the

coast, the tribe gathered bulldozers and graders, engineers and contractors. Together they brought a new industry to southeastern Connecticut, one that created thousands of jobs and millions in revenue. The tribe called it Bearclaw.

Bearclaw was a small city, housed inside what looked like a shopping mall gone mad. It sprawled over fifty acres of land, and never seemed to stop growing. The place was filled with restaurants and stores, sculptures and waterfalls. It had movie theaters and a sports arena. There was a luxury hotel and free valet parking. People came by the busload, from Boston and New York, West Virginia and Ohio, and all of them marveled at the size and sprawl carved out of the woods.

But these people would never have come for dinner and a movie, or even a waterfall. They came to place bets. The real industry at Bearclaw was gambling. Blackjack and roulette. Craps and poker. Faro and baccarat. And slot machines. Dozens, hundreds, perhaps thousands of slot machines, each of them eating rolls of coins and gaming tokens, then whistling and blinking and occasionally spitting a few coins back in return.

"This place is unbelievable," Carolina said.

"You've never been before?" Earl asked.

"No."

"I came out about a month after it opened. In '93. It was big then. I'd say it's about triple that size now."

"What did you play?"

"Blackjack, mostly. A few slots. I lost a hundred bucks. Haven't been back since."

Others were clearly not so prudent. They walked down a row of slots and watched a woman in her late fifties wearing spiked heels and sucking on a Virginia Slim. The woman blew clouds of smoke as she walked back and forth, oblivious to everything except the three one-dollar slots she serviced with a bucket of tokens. Farther down the row, a man sat staring at a machine. Every fifteen seconds he fed a new coin into the slot, then punched a button. The machine's lights flickered, then its bells chimed, but it failed to produce a paying combination. Earl and Carolina watched him for five minutes, until the man ran out of coins. He eased back from the machine, cursing and digging in his pocket.

"Could one of you guys cash a check?" he asked, noticing them. The man extended a tattered piece of paper. It was typed, and embossed with an emblem of the U.S. Government.

"Is that from Social Security?" Carolina asked.

"Yeah, so you know it's good. Come on, you want it? I don't want to give up my machine."

As Carolina and Earl walked away the man called out to a woman dressed in a skimpy outfit with a headband and a feather sticking out of her hair. The woman was pushing a cart marked CHANGE/TOKENS. She told the man he'd have to go to the casino's bank.

"Some place, eh?" Earl said.

"I can't stand it," Carolina answered.

Earl smiled tolerantly. "For most people it's a little harmless fun. What's wrong with that?"

Harmless fun. The phrase was all too familiar, and Carolina knew better.

His father had called it harmless fun. Long ago, when they lived in a comfortable home in Dubuque, Iowa. The little river city was thriving then, offering steady employment to thousands of men at the meat-packing plants and the John Deere factory or the McDonald Manufacturing company. His father had a good job on the line at Deere, building combines and tractors that would plow and plant the rolling hills of eastern Iowa and the rippling plains farther west. Across the broad expanse of the Mississippi river lay Wisconsin and Illinois. To get to them you had to cross a bridge that rolled into East Dubuque, Illinois.

East Dubuque was a blotch of a town, a mass of strip joints and bars and bait and tackle shops. It lay claim to an odd piece of history, having once been the hideout of Al Capone and other gangsters when the heat was on in Chicago. In the back rooms and alleys of the bars and clubs were a few tables for cards and dice, a few one-armed bandits, and a roulette wheel. The authorities managed to turn a blind eye to it all. The bars never closed. The games never stopped.

There were nights when his father did not come home until late, and others when he didn't come home at all.

"Where's Dad?" he would ask his mother as she stood cooking in the family's tiny kitchen. Sometimes she would tell him he was working. Later on, she wouldn't answer at all.

His parents would argue. He could hear them as he lay in bed, trying to sleep.

"Don't be telling me I can't have a night out," Joseph Carolina warned.

"We need the money," he heard his mother plead. "It was half your paycheck."

"I can make it back," Joseph said, dismissing her. "You worry too much. It's a little harmless fun."

But it was not so harmless when the bill collectors came to the door. When an eviction notice came. When the sheriff's men moved their belongings into the street. When Carolina was twelve and his father came home with a broken hand and a bloody face and refused to call the police.

A little harmless fun.

They moved toward the crap tables and the roulette wheels. There were more people, men and women, some drinking, others smoking, nearly all of them placing bets. Carolina checked his watch. Eleven twenty-five A.M.

"I never thought casinos could be so glamorous," he said.

Earl laughed. "What did you expect?"

"I don't know," Carolina said. "Something a lot sleazier. How's your gear?"

Earl carried a knapsack on his shoulder. Inside was a small eight-millimeter camera, with a lens poking from a hole in the knapsack's side. Shirley had agreed to purchase the equipment for undercover stories.

"Works fine, I guess," Earl said. "I've never used it before."

Just past the roulette wheel was a crowd of blackjack tables. Each was manned by a single dealer, dressed in a garish shirt with cheap embroidery on billowing sleeves. The dealers wore matching sashes around the waist, along with black tuxedo pants. Each table carried a sign: minimums of ten, twenty-five, fifty, and one hundred dollars.

"Research," Carolina said, "isn't going to be cheap."

They found seats at a ten-dollar table, manned by a pretty young dealer with black hair. Her nails were painted cherry red, and they flashed as her hands laid cards in front of a middle-aged woman with large hoop earrings and a black man who looked very tired.

"Hey, guys," she said, smiling. "Be with you in a second."

The two players ignored them. They were watching the cards. The dealer had a ten of clubs, and one card facedown. The woman had a two, three, and eight of diamonds showing. The black man was playing two hands, each with a face card. Each had bet the minimum.

The woman pointed at her cards. The dealer's hand flew, and a five of hearts appeared. The woman started to point again, then stopped and waved her hand.

The man pointed at one face card and drew a six. He pointed at the other and got a three. Grimacing, he pointed again. Queen of spades. The dealer quickly reached out and swept up the ten-dollar chip from the busted hand. Then she flipped her down card. Two of hearts. She drew another card. Jack of clubs. The black man grunted. The woman let out a yelp as the dealer gathered the cards and slid a ten-dollar chip to each of the players.

"So, guys," the dealer said brightly. "Want to jump in?"

"Two hundred," Carolina said, handing over a clump of bills.

Earl's eyes grew wide as the dealer counted out the chips and placed them in front of Carolina. He slid five chips over to the photographer.

"Shirley paying for this?" Earl whispered.

"Just play," Carolina said.

After fifteen minutes Carolina was up thirty dollars and Earl was down thirty.

"What am I doing wrong?" Earl said.

"You're pushing too hard," Carolina answered. "Try holding when you get sixteen or better. The dealer has to stay at fifteen, right?"

The dealer smiled. As fast as it appeared, the grin was gone, like a neon sign flashing.

"I don't know what I'm talking about, do I?" Carolina asked.

A pit boss, a young man dressed in a suit and wearing a perpetually worried expression wandered by. He looked over the dealer's shoulder and sauntered on.

"I'm not allowed to give advice," the dealer said.

Carolina looked at the badge on her shirt: Lena.

"Last time I was here I played with a guy named Tony," Carolina said. "He gave lots of advice. And I still lost."

The dealer frowned again, and began dealing another hand. The woman with the hoop earrings drew to fourteen, then busted at twenty-four. Carolina stayed at eighteen. Earl drew blackjack and let out a small growl of pleasure.

The dealer named Lena showed a nine. She flipped her hole card. A queen. She deftly slipped Carolina's ten-dollar chip away.

"Tony was a good guy, though," Carolina said. "Liked to talk about diving. You know, scuba diving?"

Lena smiled her two-second smile again. She looked at the shoe, now nearly empty.

"Time to reshuffle," she said.

The woman with the hoop rings looked disgusted. Earl shifted his knapsack. When Carolina looked at him, he winked.

"So did you know Tony?" Carolina asked.

Lena shook her head. She kept her eyes down, her hands working on breaking down the cards, spreading them and pushing them back together.

"There's three hundred dealers work this place," she said, "and I just started a couple months ago."

Carolina looked at her badge again. Next to the dealer's name was her photograph and a date. May, 1994. When he looked up again Lena was staring at him.

"Time flies when you're having fun," Carolina said.

"Are we gonna play cards or what?" the woman with the hoop earrings demanded.

Lena dealt again. The woman with the hoop rings busted again, gathered her remaining chips, and stalked off, mumbling in disgust. Carolina drew to twenty, Earl to eighteen. Lena drew to seventeen.

"It's about time I started winning," Earl said.

"I think we'd better cash in," Carolina said.

Earl looked shocked. "We're just getting started."

Carolina stood up. "Do you know where I could find Tony?"

Lena did not respond. Instead, she looked past Carolina's left shoulder at the large man in an ill-fitting mustard-colored blazer.

"Sir," the man said to Carolina, "why don't you come with us?" The blazer carried an emblem: *Security*.

Two more men in mustard blazers appeared. "You, too, sir," the first man said to Earl.

"Thanks, Lena," Carolina said. "Call me when you're in Providence sometime. We'll have lunch." Lena did not smile.

"Let's move," one of the men in blazers said. His hand tightened on Carolina's arm until it was almost painful.

"Is it okay if we bring our chips?" Earl asked.

9

The men in the mustard coats took them to an elevator and down into the casino's basement. Earl and Carolina were led into a large room, filled with dozens of television screens.

"The station doesn't have this many monitors," Earl said.

Each screen was trained on a dealer or croupier. Someone was watching every game in the casino. The overseers made notes on pieces of paper, and occasionally typed information into small computer monitors set up next to each television screen. Not one of the men and women watching the screens looked up.

Carolina and Earl were brought to a conference room. The men in the blazers relieved Earl of his knapsack. Then they were left alone.

"What'd we do?" Earl asked.

Carolina shrugged. "Maybe we didn't lose enough."

After ten minutes another man came into the room. He had graying hair and a face loaded with creases.

"My name is Parker," he said, "casino security."

"I never would have guessed," Carolina answered.

"What are you doing here?"

"We came for the Bible meeting," Carolina said.

"What?"

"I told you we were lost," Earl said to Carolina.

Parker scowled.

"Jokes are not going to get you out of here," the security man said.

"All we did was play some cards," Carolina said, "and ask a few questions."

"Why don't you ask me the questions?" Parker said.

"We're looking for information about a guy named Tony Palumbo. We heard he used to work here as a dealer. Or a croupier. Something like that."

The security man asked, "And who are you?"

Carolina told him. The security man stared. He picked up a phone.

"Bring her in."

A moment later the door opened and Lena walked in, escorted by her pit boss, who now looked more worried than ever.

"What did they talk to you about?" the security man demanded.

"That one." Lena pointed a red-tipped finger at Earl. "He didn't say anything. The other one kept asking about Tony."

"What did he ask?"

"Diving stuff. How Tony liked to dive. Nothing about the counting—"

The security man put up a hand to silence her.

"How'd they do?"

"Pretty even," Lena said, "they won a little and lost a little."

"Well," Carolina said, "you didn't give us much of a chance."

Another man in a blazer came in and whispered in Parker's ear, then left.

"What was the camera for?" he asked.

Carolina looked at them, the security man asking questions, the pit boss who acted like he had indigestion, and the young dealer looking scared to death.

"Like I said," Carolina answered, "we wanted to know about Tony Palumbo. He said he had this great thing going down at the tables down in Bearclaw, with a girl named Lena that he went to high school with in Cranston."

Lena gasped. "That's bullshit. I barely knew Tony, and he told me he was from Westerly, I swear—"

"Shut up," the security man said, flushing. He looked at the pit boss. "Get out of here." The pit boss hustled Lena out of the room. She threw Carolina an angry look.

"You're trespassing on tribal property," Parker said. "We have your pictures. If you show up here again, we'll have you arrested."

"I'm crushed," Carolina said.

"What about our camera?" Earl asked.

"Have your station contact us," Parker said. "You're not getting it back today."

Parker stood up. The door opened again, and more men in mustard blazers appeared.

"Let's go," one of them said.

"Fine," Carolina said, "but first tell us where we can cash in."

The men in mustard blazers followed Earl and Carolina to their van, and drove behind them until they reached the edge of the Bearclaw property.

Carolina waved as they drove off. The gesture was not returned.

"Pissy, aren't they?"

"Not half as bad as Shirley's gonna be," Earl said.

"What makes you say that?"

"For one thing, we got in trouble again. For another, we don't have shit by way of a story."

"Earl," Carolina said, "you've got to look at the glass as half full, not half empty."

Earl looked at him as if he were deranged. Carolina pretended not to notice.

"That dealer said that Palumbo came from Westerly, right?"

"So?" Earl said.

"So let's pay a little visit."

"You don't think we should check in with the station?"

"Why, so she can pull us off to work on something else? After Bearclaw, we may not get down this way again."

"I won't argue with you there," Earl said. "But Westerly's got thirty thousand people in it. Where do you want to start?"

* * *

They started with the yellow pages. Carolina found three shops listed that sold diving equipment. The first was a sporting goods store with only a few masks and fins on the shelves. The manager had never heard of Tony Palumbo. A second store had gone out of business.

The third was found by a fishing pier and marina. The place was little more than a shack, built of tarpaper and wood turned gray from years of salt air and Atlantic breeze. A sign by the door read FRANK'S DIVE SHOP in chipped red letters. Carolina left Earl in the van.

The inside of the shop was jammed with air regulators and wet suits, fins and air tanks. A teenaged boy was looking over a selection of masks when Carolina walked in. After a minute he went outside.

The lone clerk looked to be about forty. He was working on an air regulator.

"Are you Frank?" Carolina asked.

The man looked up. He did not smile, but his expression brightened. "Sure am. Can I help you?"

"I'm looking for information."

"About diving?"

"About a diver. His name was Tony Palumbo."

The man named Frank turned his attention back to the regulator.

"Who are you?"

"My name is Michael Carolina."

"You a cop?"

"I work for Channel Three."

The man didn't say anything. Carolina stood and waited, the silence growing more and more awkward. The man finally put the regulator down. With nothing else to divert his attention, he looked back at Carolina.

"I have no idea what Tony was doing up in Providence. I already told the police that."

"What police?"

"The feds. ATF or whatever. They were here a couple days ago. Came by with a couple Westerly cops."

"How did you know Tony?"

"He practically grew up here. Hell, I hired him to work during the summers when he was in high school."

"What did the police want?"

"What he was doing up in that cove. Same thing you want, right?"

"Right." Carolina didn't know what to make of the man. He was pleasant enough, and he seemed to know what he was talking about. But something wasn't right.

"You must be pretty upset," Carolina said.

"Why's that?"

"Well, your friend died, the police are investigating—"

"Did I say he was my friend?"

"I just assumed—"

"You assumed wrong." Frank shook his head. "Maybe once, when he was a kid, we were friends. But when Tony Palumbo died he was a junkie and a liar, and he'd steal from you as soon as look at you."

"Those are pretty harsh words."

"You think so? The guy broke into my shop a few years back, looking for gear to sell to get a fix. I knew it was him. Told him I'd get the cops on him if he didn't leave me alone."

"Why didn't you?"

The man looked around for a minute, hesitating. He walked over to a stack of boxes and began putting them on a shelf. Carolina decided to switch gears.

"I heard Tony was in the SEALs."

Frank looked up. "That's a lot of crap. He used to tell people that, try to impress them. He joined the navy after high school all right. But I heard he washed out. General discharge, not even honorable. Right after, that's when he came home, started getting mixed up with that smack and everything."

"How'd he support himself?"

"I heard he was trying to do some commercial diving. But that's real competitive work, and there isn't much to go around. He never caught on. At least, not that I knew of."

"How'd he wind up at Bearclaw?"

Frank snorted. "Hell, half of Connecticut and Rhode Island wound up at Bearclaw. That's the biggest employer in the area since EB started losing work."

"So how'd he get fired?"

"I don't know. But there are rumors."

"Like what?"

"Like he got involved in capping."

"Capping?"

"Yeah, it's a blackjack scam. See, when you lay a bet down there, you do it before you get any cards. Then the dealer gives you one. It's illegal to bet after that."

"Okay," Carolina said.

"But with capping, the dealer looks away for a second. When he does, depending on the card you draw, say a face card or an ace, you increase your bet."

"What does that do?"

Frank snorted. "You don't play cards much, do you?"

"No."

"If you're any kind of card player, once you know one of your cards, you increase the odds on winning. The word is there was a group of dealers capping for some bookies out of Providence. They were taking two, three thousand dollars out of the casino every night. Then the dealers got caught by one of them security cameras."

"Why weren't they arrested?"

"Bearclaw didn't want the publicity. The dealers got fired."

"When was the last time you saw Tony?"

"Couple weeks ago. He used to hang out down on the pier. I'd see him walking around. Then one day he walked in and bought a new tank and a regulator. Paid cash."

"Do you know where he got the money?"

"I didn't know, and I didn't care. A customer's a customer, so I took his money."

"Listen, Mr.—"

"Terranova. Frank Terranova."

They shook hands. "You've been very helpful."

Frank Terranova shrugged. "I still don't know what he was doing in that cove."

"Neither do I," said Carolina.

"I'll tell you one thing, though. If it was Tony, you can bet it wasn't good."

Earl was napping in the passenger seat when Carolina came out. He looked at the photographer, then walked down the pier in search of a phone.

"I've been wondering where you were," Shirley said.

"Oh, we've had a wonderful day." Carolina briefly described their eviction from the casino and his conversation with the dive shop owner. Shirley was unimpressed.

"So you have no tape? No package?"

"Doesn't look that way. What about your other stories?"

"One of them fell through. We have a six o'clock show and two stories."

Carolina knew it was best to keep quiet.

"I need you to get back here," Shirley said. "Maybe there's a live shot we can have you do."

"I'm on my way."

He hung up the phone and started back to the car. Carolina was genuinely sympathetic to Shirley's problem. The pressure to put together a decent broadcast with a shorthanded staff was enormous. Still, it was impossible to investigate things like the background of Tony Palumbo and still focus on the breaking stories of the day.

A reporter's biggest enemy, he'd long ago concluded, was time.

This was especially true in a tight economy. The reason so many stories went unreported was because there wasn't enough time to dig them all out.

Carolina was so wrapped up in his thoughts that he almost forgot to stop to look at some of the boats along the pier. There was a lean white sailboat, rocking gently against a set of fenders. It looked out of place next to a pair of rusted commercial fishing boats, their gear spread out across their decks, drying in the afternoon sun.

But the thing that made Carolina scramble for a pen was the registration number poking out of the back of a purple cigarette boat, painted in yellow letters, just above the hideous name BREAKING WIND.

10

The Department of Environmental Management's boating division was closing when Carolina called.

"Try calling back tomorrow," said the person answering the phone.

"It's very important, couldn't I get it from you today?"

The state worker at the other end of the line sighed and relented.

"I show a listing for a Thelma Pitts, 225 Elmwood Avenue, Cranston."

Carolina thanked her and hung up.

"It's the same boat I saw last night," he said to Shirley.

"Good," she said. "Now, about this live shot. I think you're going to like this—"

Carolina groaned. Shirley ignored it.

"It's about the pieces of wood they found in Stillhouse Cove. Those people from the historical society, and that environmental group . . . what's it called again?" Shirley looked down at some notes.

"Save the Chowder," Carolina said.

"Save the Chowder, that's it. They're demonstrating on the State House steps tonight."

"What for?"

"They're trying to push someone in government into declaring Stillhouse Cove off-limits to boats."

"Didn't they do this yesterday?"

"They're doing it again tonight," Shirley said.

"And you want this as a live shot?"

"Have you got anything better?" Shirley snapped. "Listen, Michael, I've humored you all day. But I need a body out there tonight. They'll light some candles, maybe throw up a few signs. You talk about why they're there, what they want. We roll a little tape of the waterfront from a few days ago. I'll make sure the editor shows some of that wood being lifted out of the water. We come back to you, you wrap it up and throw it back to the studio. You could do this in your sleep."

"That's what most of our audience will be doing."

Shirley looked ready to commit murder.

"All right, all right. Sorry."

The tension in the news director's office eased somewhat. Shirley lit a cigarette.

"Before you go," she said, "I want you to know I appreciate your help."

"Thanks."

"How are things with Marie?"

"They're not."

"Oh." Shirley looked around, trying to think of another subject.

"She said I was too normal," Carolina said.

"Really?"

"Yeah, she's seeing some guy who does performance art with cucumbers and finger paint."

"If that's her taste, then I guess you are too normal."

Carolina turned to go.

"Why don't you give me the name of the person who owns that boat?" Shirley asked.

Carolina did. "What are you going to do?"

"Just an idea. Call me after you finish up."

People in the trenches of broadcast news have a name for the sort of story Shirley wanted: a Revlon live shot. The term meant that the story had "the look, the feel" of an important piece of news when in fact it was little more than makeup.

That evening's Revlon live shot went exactly the way Shirley predicted, at least until the end.

A small group of demonstrators appeared outside the State House. They marched up and down the steps, chanting, "Save the Ship, Save the Cove." Some carried signs. Others held candles, even though it was summer and the sun had not yet set. Garrison Pinker and his tweeds were not in attendance, but Sally Generous showed up with a bullhorn to cheer on the troops.

Carolina spoke for a minute. He let the camera pan across the crowd of demonstrators and the smattering of people who gathered to watch them. The station rolled some tape. Then the camera came back to Carolina, who promptly tossed back to the studio.

"Is there any evidence linking the explosion to the clams?" the station's anchor asked.

"None that I know of, Dave," Carolina said.

"Then, why are we covering this?"

Carolina looked around at the demonstrators.

"I guess because they have candles and signs and there isn't much else going on, Dave."

The photographer assigned to the live shot doubled over in laughter.

"I can't believe you said that."

"I can't believe he asked," Carolina said.

The cell phone in the station's microwave van rang. The technician, still cracking up, handed it to Carolina.

"What the fuck is the matter with you?" Shirley demanded.

"He asked me a question. What was I supposed to say?"

"He's an anchor, Michael. That means he's an idiot almost by definition. You're supposed to be able to finesse this sort of thing."

"Actually," Carolina said, "I thought it was a pretty good question."

"I ought to suspend you right now."

"Come on, it wasn't that bad."

"You haul your ass back here. I want you in my office as soon as the show's over."

"She pretty mad?" the technician asked when Carolina hung up.

"You could say that."

The microwave technician and photographer watched as Carolina jumped into a car for the short drive back to the station.

"We gotta get that on the gag reel," the tech said.

"I'll tell you one thing," the photographer said, "that's the last time Shirley sends him out on a Revlon."

"You bastard."

"Shirley, I'm sorry."

"That was humiliating."

"I didn't mean it to be."

"Of all the people in this place, you ought to know how important it is for a news organization to maintain its credibility."

"I do know," Carolina said. "And I'm sorry I embarrassed you. But the problem is we don't have enough staff to do this right."

"That's not my fault," Shirley said. "The GM cut our budget this year."

"I know, and he still expects miracles. But when you first hired me you said I'd have the time to work on things in-depth. I don't mind helping out when something's breaking, but tonight . . . Well, that was ridiculous."

Shirley gave him a long look.

"You're a very smart guy, Michael," she said, reaching for a cigarette. "You know I like you. But sometimes you get so wrapped up in what you're doing you lose sight of other things that are still important."

"Such as?"

"Such as those people out there on the State House steps. I know you think Garrison Pinker is a stuffed shirt. And you probably think Sally Generous is just another hippie wannabe with sandals and hairy legs."

"Well, aren't they?" Carolina said, smiling. Shirley was not amused.

"Sally has been one of the driving forces in Rhode Island on aquaculture for years."

"And what, may I ask, is aquaculture?"

"Clam farming. Oyster farming. Around here it's mostly clams. Preserving them and growing them for future generations. There's a lot of hostility between the hunters and farmers."

Carolina raised an eyebrow. Shirley sighed.

"Quahoggers," she said, "are hunters. They dig the clam beds hunting for clams. Aquaculture is all about farming. Growing the clams, feeding them, protecting them, and then harvesting, just like you would with an acre of corn. I'm not an expert on the subject, but apparently that's what this whole Save the Chowder thing is all about."

"Why didn't you tell me that before?"

"What, me tell my best reporter how to do his job?" Shirley said in mock horror. "I assumed you would figure it out on your own."

"She was so abrasive—"

"Yes, she is. And she does a lousy job of making her point. The problem is, she's still got a point to make."

Now Carolina was quiet for a moment.

"Since I appear to have humbled you," Shirley said, "there's something you should know. While you were out getting ready for that live shot, I did a little research."

"On what?"

"This lady Thelma Pitts, the one DEM says owns that speedboat." Shirley laid a hand on a telephone cross-reference directory and tapped her finger. "There's no address in here for Thelma Pitts. But the address DEM has belongs to someone else in Cranston."

"Who?"

"Actually, it's a company. Whipple Realty."

* * *

Carolina took another drive to Edgewood that evening. Shirley went along.

"It's so pretty down here," she said. "I love these houses."

Carolina didn't answer. He was counting the number of Whipple Realty signs. There were more than a dozen planted in the yards of various homes that ringed Stillhouse Cove. Whipple Realty had a stranglehold on the neighborhood.

"Has it occurred to you that virtually every house in this area is for sale or has been sold?" Carolina asked.

"I wonder," Shirley said. "I bet you could get some great bargains down here."

"Maybe."

"You think something's going on," Shirley said, looking at him. Carolina turned a corner and went up a hill. Then he pulled the car into a driveway, backed up, and turned around.

"I don't know what to think."

"How do you like your new place?"

"It's all right," he said, cruising back down the hill.

"Not like living on a boat, I'll bet."

"Not at all. I miss that."

"How are you doing with the breakup thing?"

"I haven't given it much thought," Carolina lied.

"Don't get me wrong," Shirley said, "Marie is very pretty, and I'm sure she's fun to be with, but she never struck me as your type."

"Oh? And what's my type?"

Shirley did not immediately respond.

"Someone normal?"

"Excuse me?" Shirley said.

"Never mind," Carolina responded.

Shirley's expression turned from quizzical to bemused. Carolina did not look at her, but swung the car back onto Narragansett Boulevard, heading toward Providence.

"Well," she said, "what do you want to do about this real estate company?"

"I think I want to find out why they have so many listings down here."

"And how do you intend to do that?"

"I'd like your help," Carolina said, and he told her.

11

The morning sun burned hot and hard, promising to bake Rhode Island and its citizens the whole day long. By mid-morning the thermometers were pushing into the nineties, with little hint of a breeze to provide relief.

Whipple Realty was housed in a nondescript storefront off Elmwood Avenue. The front door's paint was peeling, and the windows were in need of a wash. A set of lawn signs lay piled against one wall, and the lone steelcase desk in the room was piled with paper.

"At least it's cool," Shirley whispered, eyeing a rust-colored air conditioner rattling noisily from a perch on a side window. The two of them stood there for a minute, letting the rush of freon spill over them.

"Anybody here?" Carolina called after a minute.

A toilet flushed, and steps could be heard coming from a back hall. A slender woman with a hatchet face and prematurely gray hair appeared, surprised at the customers in her office.

"We didn't mean to startle you," Shirley said.

"That's all right." The woman pulled a cigarette to her mouth and inhaled deeply. She set the cigarette in an ashtray on her desk and hugged herself unconsciously.

"Can I help you?"

"Yes," Shirley said.

"Buying or selling?" The woman was growing more eager.

"Well, right now we're just looking."

And so was the realtor. Her eyes were playing over the two of them, taking in their clothes, Shirley's jewelry, the way they carried themselves. Finally, the woman picked up the cigarette again with her left hand and stuck out her right.

"I'm Molly Whipple," she said.

"Shirley Templeton." The two women shook hands firmly. Shirley pointed at Carolina. "This is my friend, Michael."

Carolina nodded politely. The woman took another deep drag, then blew smoke all over the room.

"Have we met?" she asked.

"I don't think so," Carolina said.

"I know you from somewhere."

Carolina smiled and shrugged.

"We were interested in some residential property," Shirley said.

"I have some wonderful things in Edgewood." The woman pulled a large fiberboard from beside the desk, covered with photographs of houses.

"What price range were you interested in?" she asked, trying to sound matter-of-fact. She never took her eyes from Shirley.

"Well, we're not really sure yet." Shirley smiled. "We want to see what's out there."

"Of course," Molly Whipple said. "This is a beautiful Victorian, just got the listing last week, four bedrooms, two baths, near a school. You have children?"

Shirley ignored the question. "Is it on the water?"

"Oh, just a few minutes away."

"What about air-conditioning?" Carolina asked.

"This is Edgewood," Whipple said. She smiled, revealing a set of tobacco-stained teeth. "We get the breeze in Edgewood."

Carolina pointedly looked at the air conditioner, still rattling away, then smiled back. "Is that a no?"

The woman snubbed out her cigarette and lit another. She turned back to Shirley.

"I'm sorry, what price range did you say again?"

"We were looking for something near the water," Shirley said. "Perhaps in the area of Stillhouse Cove."

"Oh, that's too bad," Whipple said. "I don't have anything there right now."

"You don't?"

"I have some wonderful properties down near Pawtuxet Cove, and more near Columbia Avenue." The realtor pointed at another house. "This is a pretty little duplex, a little run-down, but for the right kind of person, it produces a lot of income. Are you good with your hands?" She looked at Carolina.

"Depends on what I'm doing," Carolina said.

"Why don't you just tell me what you're looking for?"

"We really were looking for something on the water," Shirley answered. "And I don't understand. We've been down to Stillhouse Cove, and your signs are everywhere. You must have sold half a dozen houses."

"Oh, I have listings there," the woman said. "But they go very quickly. I've sold places there in less than a day. And right now"—she inhaled once again—"there just isn't anything available."

The woman was hugging herself again.

"May I use your bathroom?" Shirley asked. The woman pointed toward the back hallway. "The door sticks," she said.

"I'll hold it shut," Shirley answered.

The woman looked at Carolina. He picked up the fiberboard and pretended to look through the properties.

"By any chance," he asked, "are you related to Abraham Whipple?"

Molly Whipple brightened. "He's a distant relative," she said. "You're familiar with the story?"

"I just heard about the *Gaspee* a few days ago," Carolina said. "Quite a tale."

"Yes, he was a true patriot."

"When he wasn't running slaves for the Browns," Carolina said.

"Excuse me?"

"Nothing. Is the real estate business competitive around here?"

"Very."

Carolina set the board down again next to the woman's desk.

"Maybe you know an acquaintance of mine," he said.

"Who's that?"

"A lady named Thelma Pitts."

Molly Whipple's face went as blank as if someone had drawn an eraser across it.

"I've never heard of her."

"Really? Are you the only realtor in this office?"

"Yes."

"Well," Carolina said, "there must be a lot of realtors in Rhode Island."

"There are. How do you know her?"

"A mutual friend," Carolina said.

"Now I know who you are," the woman said. "You're that guy from TV."

"It's so nice to meet a viewer," Carolina said.

"Why are you here?"

"We wanted to ask you about some property. Specifically, we want to know why you have every listing in Stillhouse Cove, but you have nothing for sale."

"Where's your friend?" The woman looked around. In a moment Shirley stepped out from the hallway.

"Where were you?" the woman demanded.

"Powdering my nose," Shirley said innocently.

"The toilet didn't flush."

"You weren't listening."

"You're not buying any property."

"I never said we were," Shirley said. "I told you we were just looking. You drew your own conclusions."

The woman was no longer smiling. Her cigarette festered in the ashtray, sending a thin blue line toward the ceiling.

"You'd better leave."

"You mean you don't want us on your mailing list?" Carolina asked.

"Get out."

They were back on the street in thirty seconds.

"That's one nasty lady," Carolina said.

"I agree," Shirley said. "Realtors frequently are."

"I'd like to know what she's up to."

Shirley smiled. "I think I may have a hint."

The woman who called herself Molly Whipple lit another cigarette, then dialed Jimmy Flannery. He greeted her informally.

"What?"

"That reporter, the one from Channel Three, he just came by."

"So?"

"So he was with some broad, and they pretended they wanted
to buy a house, but they only wanted to look around the cove."

Jimmy was silent for a few seconds.

"I told them we didn't have nothing."

Jimmy was silent again, and this was something the woman did
not like. The quiet was worse than torture.

"Is this going to be a problem?" Jimmy asked, finally.

"I don't know. They asked an awful lot of questions. And the
guy was asking about Thelma Pitts."

"Ah, shit," Jimmy said.

"They know something, Jimmy, they know something."

The woman blew more smoke through her nose. It formed a
gray patch around her face and hair.

"The fuck you want me to do?" Jimmy asked.

"I don't know. You want me to do something?"

"No," Jimmy said, "not the kinda thing you got in mind. Couple years ago some guys of mine laid into this guy outside the Tattoo. Put him in the hospital. Know what? It didn't do nothin'. Just
made him work harder."

"You could take him out."

"Yeah, and have a fuckin' news media martyr? That'll leave us
with fifty people lookin' around. No thanks."

"So we just sit here?"

"No, we try to find the fuckin' clamdigger, like I said before.

This other guy, he's asking questions, but you didn't give him no answers, right?"

"Of course not," the woman said, inhaling again. She looked around the office, wondering about Shirley's visit to the rest room.

"Well, if all he's doing is asking questions, and he don't have no answers, he ain't got much of a story. Right?"

"Right." The woman wanted to hang up now. She needed to check the back office. Besides, she didn't like his tone. It was very calm, short, the way he got when he was very mad. The woman didn't like it when Jimmy got mad. Once, she heard, the man had nearly strangled his own brother for saying something Jimmy didn't care for.

"One more thing," Jimmy said.

"What's that?" The woman ached to hang up.

"I don't want no more calls. Not until you got something to tell me."

"Okay, Jimmy."

Jimmy paused. The woman's frustration at not being able to end the call was such that she actually felt pain in her stomach. But Jimmy did not hang up. He waited in silence, almost as if he were enjoying her suffering.

"Something good," he said.

"Okay, Jimmy, okay."

Finally, he ended the call. The woman put the phone down and walked back into the hallway. The door to the bathroom was closed, and she went past it, into the back office filled with file cabinets and another steelcase desk. There were more documents on the desk, most piled neatly on the corners, a few scattered on the center of a worn blotter. So much paper, it was hard to keep track of it all.

She spent twenty minutes going through it, leafing through the pages, looking at the stationery and the bills, before she decided she could not tell whether anything was missing.

* * *

"So what do you make of this?"

They were back in Shirley's office. The paper Shirley held in her hand had the feel of ancient parchment. But the edges were too clean, the corners too crisp, for the document to be old. It was new paper, washed and treated to look old. On it, there were two words: GASPEE GALLERY.

"Looks like a piece of stationery," Carolina said.

"I think you're right," Shirley said, running her hand over it. "Where did you find it?"

"She had a pile of documents on her desk. I didn't want to grab anything she'd miss."

"Did you notice anything else?" Carolina asked.

"In the papers? Not really. Just a lot of figures and some deeds, purchase and sales agreements, things like that."

"You've got a lot of balls," Carolina said.

Shirley gave a little shrug. "I was a reporter once, too."

"Not many reporters would do what you did."

"You would."

"Maybe."

"So," Shirley said, "what do we do with it?"

They both looked at the paper. "I have no idea," Carolina said. "I guess we keep digging."

The needle on the gauge hovered just to the right of the letter "E." It had been there for more than two days, and Mitty knew it would not linger much longer. A few more miles, maybe, then it would slip a little more to the left and his battered truck would go no farther. Not without a drink of gas, anyway.

The sun was high in the sky, the air thick with humidity and the fumes of truck exhaust and rotting clams. Mitty nudged his vehicle along the side of the road, coming to a stop near an old gray shack.

The shack was located just outside the village called Wickford, part of the larger municipality known as North Kingstown. Wickford was a charming little place halfway up the western side of Narragansett Bay, and the shack looked out of character there, like something the tide washed in, then out and back in again.

Mitty usually did not venture so far south of Warwick. But heat, desperation, and a truckload of lukewarm shellfish would drive a man to do all kinds of strange things.

He was sweaty and thirsty from the ride in the truck; the air-conditioning had died long ago. He was hungry, too, hungry for anything but clams. They were all he'd eaten for the last week, eaten them steamed in a little pot he used to cook near the beach. He was down to a few matches, a can of propane, and a couple of dollars. That and the buckets of clams in the truck bed, oozing warmly in the summer heat.

The clam shack was closed in the winters, and shut down occasionally in the summer when the owner forgot to pay off a health inspector. Today it was open, and Mitty knew the owner might be willing to take a few buckets of dirty quahogs and throw a few dollars his way in return. To Mitty, contamination didn't matter: the clams were headed for the deep fryer or the chowder pot and no one would ever know.

He reached into the truck bed and grabbed a handle, hauling the clam bucket out, letting it swing at his side. Mitty shuffled past the picnic tables, lined up under a flimsy tin awning. There were few customers, just a mother with a few children eating clam rolls, and two guys in designer sweatsuits drinking soda. Mitty paid them no mind. He scuffed his beat-up work shoes on the gravel as he lugged the clam bucket up to a grease-stained window. He peered through at a sweaty man wearing cutoffs, undershirt, and dirty apron.

"Wanna buy some clams?" Mitty mumbled.

The man was cutting onions for chowder. He paused to wipe his brow with a bare hand, then went back to slicing.

" 'Dey fresh?"

"Right from the bay," Mitty said, hoisting the bucket.

The man did not look at him. Instead he glanced out at the tables with his customers.

"Geddafuggout, I could smell your truck comin' a mile down the road."

Mitty did not blink. He'd heard the line before.

"I'm tellin' yas, they're good clams."

The man was still sweating. He looked up again, but past Mitty, not at him.

"Boil these suckers up, make chowder, fry 'em 'til they stop movin', and stick 'em in a roll. Come on, I sell yas ten buckets for twenty-five dollars."

"Screw."

"Okay, twenty."

The man was still not looking at him. Mitty felt uneasy. He needed money for gas and a little food, and his stomach hurt from eating so many clams. His mind wandered as he pictured a glass of cold beer.

"I said I ain't innarested," the man in the greasy window said. He sounded nervous.

"Listen," Mitty said. "Yer robbin' me here, but I'll give ya all the buckets for fifteen dollars, okay?"

"You need money, Mitty?"

The bushy little clamdigger did a slow turn to take in the two men who stood behind him. They were the same ones who were drinking soda at the shack just a few moments before.

"We can take the clams off your hands, pal," one of them said, smiling, his eyes hidden behind a pair of Vuarnets.

Mitty recognized them now. Their sweatsuits were unzipped to the waist, revealing hairy stomachs and matching sets of gold chains. The same outfits they wore a few nights ago on the water, when they were driving a cigarette boat called *Breaking Wind*.

"Mitty," one of them said, "we got a friend still wants to talk to you." The man patted his hip. Mitty noticed a small bulge. "And he don't like hearing anyone say no."

Mitty's head felt swollen from the heat, the thickness of the air, and the odor of the buckets. But his feeble brain could still tell him that the two men were trouble. This was the reason no one would buy his clams. The men must have visited every fish market and restaurant in the West Bay. Waited and watched for Mitty and his clams.

One of the men reached for a bucket. Mitty pulled away, hauled back, and swung. The load of clams was heavy, perhaps twenty pounds, and Mitty's arms were powerful, built up from years of raking and pulling and digging and throwing. The bucket hit the first goombah full in the face. There was a nasty sound, of hard plastic making contact with nose cartilage.

The man let out a gasp and instinctively put up a hand. Mitty switched his gaze to the other goombah, the one who'd touched his side. The man was tugging at the waistband on his sweatsuit. Reaching for that bulge Mitty had seen before. The clamdigger pulled his bucket back again, then heaved for all he was worth. This time he let the bucket go.

The man was awash in filthy brine and rotting clams. The force was enough to knock his sunglasses off. Mitty didn't stop to look. He turned and bolted for his truck.

The two goombahs began to recover. They both looked at Navel as he reached his truck and opened the door. The drenched man finally pulled the bulge from his waistband: a .38 revolver. He started to run toward Mitty. The other goombah, tears streaming past his broken nose, followed. Navel reached into the truck, grabbing a battered lighter in one hand and a red stick in the other.

The goombah with the gun froze. His buddy, still half-blind from the tears and the swelling on his face, crashed into him.

Mitty wore a look of absolute panic. He flicked the lighter and a flame spit out.

"The fuck are you doing?" the man with the gun demanded.

Mitty didn't say a word.

The woman with the children saw what Navel was holding and let out a small shriek. She grabbed her children and stood up, spilling pink lemonade and fried clams all over her picnic table. The owner of the clam shack peered outside.

"You fuckin' crazy?" the gunman shouted again. He held on to the gun, weighing his chances.

"Back off," Mitty said. "Back the fug off."

The woman with her children was pulling her kids away from the picnic tables, dragging them down the gravel lane. A few cars passed by, but none stopped or slowed enough to see what was happening. Mitty continued to hold the lighter in his hand. The hand with the dynamite stick didn't move.

The goombah with the newly broken nose wheezed loudly, but said nothing. In the silence, however, the gunman was growing cocky.

"What's your problem, Mitty? All we want is to ask a few questions."

"I said back off," Mitty answered.

The heat rippled off the flame in Mitty's hand. It was so heavy, so thick. Mitty stood in front of his truck and looked at the men, trying not to think about breathing.

The gunman dropped his .38 to his side. Then he shrugged, giving in.

"Okay, Mitty, okay. You want us to back off?" He took a step back and shrugged again. "Okay. We go."

Mitty sighed. He looked down at his hand.

The flame from the lighter went out.

The gunman saw it the same time that Mitty did. He grinned quickly and pointed his .38 again, this time at Mitty's hand. Real smart. It was a short shot to shoot the lighter away.

There was a dry snap, metal hitting metal. Then another. The man pulled the trigger again, but the .38 was simply too wet.

Mitty rolled his finger along the lighter again. This time the flint caught. The flame sprang up.

Mitty didn't remember the events that followed with any significant degree of clarity. There was just so much going on . . . The dynamite stick rolling gently toward the screaming gunman and his partner, who managed to pick the thing up and throw it away. The stick traveling in a high arc, then falling next to the shack. The sweaty owner running, his brow screwed up, his mouth open, and his arms waving. And Mitty jumping into his truck, nursing it back down the road away from the blown building covered in flames and smoke and the smell of burned chowder.

12

Bert Schumacher realized he had a serious problem.

It was bad enough that the clam shack was nothing more than charred splinters, that the picnic tables had been destroyed or blown fifty yards away, that the shack owner was babbling incoherently about a short, bearded man with a bucket of clams and a stick of dynamite.

The real problem was the media. And his partner Ernie. And the combination of the two. They were driving him nuts.

Ernie O'Mara was in all his glory, holding an impromptu press conference for a gaggle of TV cameras and newspapers.

"What led to the explosion?" one of the TV reporters asked.

"Our best information," Ernie said, swelling with pride, "was that there was a dispute over clam prices with a clam wholesaler and some customers."

"Don't you mean the owner?" another reporter asked. "I mean, why would a quahogger fight with a customer?"

"We're looking into that," Ernie said, "we're pursuing all leads."

"Does this case have anything to do with the explosion up in Stillhouse Cove?"

"As I said," Ernie sighed, "this investigation is still ongoing, but it certainly looks that way, doesn't it?"

"Ah, shit," Bert muttered. First chance I get, he thought, I'm gonna recommend they ship this guy to the ATF field office in Sioux Falls.

"What did you say your name was again?" a female reporter asked.

"O'Mara. Special Agent Ernest O'Mara, Providence Office."

"Excuse me, Agent O'Mara, could I have a word with you?"

"Be with you in a moment," Ernie said, nodding gravely in Bert's direction. "Ladies and gentlemen, I really have to get back to work."

"Agent O'Mara, do you have any idea who you're dealing with?" The question came from a Providence *Herald* reporter, a veteran journalist who recognized O'Mara for what he was but couldn't resist the opportunity to get a good quote.

Ernie quickly rose to the bait.

"I think it's clear that we're dealing with a madman. This, this—clamcake bomber—is completely out of control."

The reporters were experiencing journalistic orgasm—a headline quote that would resonate for days. Hell, it might even make the national papers or the networks. Bert, however, was not amused.

"Hey, partner," he said through his teeth, "you're the one who's crazy."

Ernie looked hurt. "Come on, Bert. They just wanted some information."

"Then let them call Boston. You know we're not supposed to talk to the press."

"You talked to Carolina," Ernie said, petulant.

"I traded information. And when I talked, it wasn't on-camera. 'Madman.' You must have clam shit for brains."

"You think I'm in trouble?"

"Hell, I don't know. Why don't you go do something useful, like see if the owner's calm enough to make a decent statement."

"I dunno, Bert, he's pretty upset. It's the guy's livelihood."

Bert snorted. "You ever eat here? I did, once. Had trots for a week. The bomber did Rhode Island a favor."

Ernie went off in search of the owner, while Bert watched a fire company move in to hose down the remains of the shack. The water kicked up steam that shimmered in the swollen heat. Bert wiped his brow and squinted, trying to keep sweat from dripping into his eyes. Then he opened them and frowned.

"Not you again."

"Is that any way to greet an old friend?" Carolina said.

"I don't have any comment," Bert said, and turned to walk away. Carolina stepped in front of him.

"You want Ernie to be your agency's spokesman tonight on Channel Three?"

"I don't know what you're talking about. Besides, there's nothing I can do about him anyway."

"Sure you can."

"I don't do on-camera stuff."

"So tell me something off-camera."

"Why? You'll just use the crap Ernie gave to the other reporters."

Carolina chuckled. "Well, what do you expect me to do with a line like clamcake bomber? Tell you what. Give me something straight on this thing, I'll attribute it to a source close to the investigation. Do that, and I keep the other comments your partner makes to a minimum."

Bert Schumacher looked at the reporter. "You know," he said, "I don't like you much."

"I know," Carolina answered. "I don't like you much either."

"As long as we understand each other," Bert said.

Carolina kept his word.

The Channel Three story at six o'clock contained video from the bomb scene, and a babbling sound bite from the clam-shack owner. Ernie also made the cut with his remark about the clamcake bomber. But the exclusive angle to the story was about the source of the explosion.

"Sources close to this investigation," Carolina said, "believe that the dynamite used in today's bombing came from the same lot used in last week's explosion at Stillhouse Cove, injuring a diver and causing extensive damage to a marina. Authorities believe all of the dynamite was stolen two weeks ago from a construction site on the Providence waterfront."

The microwave van's cell phone was ringing seconds after Carolina threw back to the station.

"That was nice about the dynamite," Shirley said.

"Thanks," Carolina replied.

"What about the dispute over the price of the clams?"

"That's bullshit," Carolina said.

"The other reporters had it."

"The other reporters," Carolina said, "would say pigs fly if they got the right sound bite."

"Are you telling me we have the same sound from O'Mara?"

"We do," Carolina said, "but I wouldn't trust Ernie O'Mara any farther than I could throw him."

Journalists as a rule are an insecure lot, always worried about beating the competition, and being beaten in return. But the only thing worse than being beaten is being wrong. Carolina knew that. So did Shirley. She broke the tension with a laugh.

"Well," she said, "come on back. Make sure you give your video to the eleven o'clock producer."

The live truck operators were almost finished breaking down the equipment. Some of the other reporters had already left.

"I almost forgot," Shirley said. "There's a message here for you. Carla Tattaglia. Wants you to call."

Carolina took the number, hung up, then dialed again.

"Hello," Carla said.

"Uh, it's Michael Carolina."

"Hot day to be covering explosions."

"Better than being in one."

"I suppose that's true," Carla said. There was something in her voice he had not heard before. He couldn't decide what, but it was—pleasant.

"So where are you?"

"I'm at home," she said. "But I was wondering if you might like to get some dinner with me." She said it so calmly, so innocently, it caught him by surprise.

"Sure."

"When do you want to meet?" Carla asked.

Carolina looked around. The truck operator was done, and Earl was standing by his car. They both looked like they were waiting for him to finish so they could go home.

"I've got to go back to the station, first. Say an hour?"

"Great." She gave him the name of an Italian restaurant in Johnston, just outside Providence.

"Is this business or pleasure?" Carolina asked before he hung up.

"We'll see," Carla said. "Maybe both."

The restaurant was in a strip mall, guarded on one side by Angelina's Beauty Shop and on the other by Capuano Insurance. The place was crowded, filled with happy, laughing people enjoying a night out. Candles burned at each table, casting flickering lights on watercolor prints of Venice and Rome. Despite the air-conditioning, Carolina could smell warm bread and garlic.

A hostess showed him to a table and handed him a menu and wine list. He was still looking at the entrees when he realized someone was standing next to him.

She looked thinner without the uniform. Her dark hair was swirling past her shoulders, touching the top of a freshly pressed denim button-down, which was tucked into a skirt decorated with a floral print. Her legs were bare, except for a pair of sandals. She looked . . . clean. Carolina stood up.

"Hello, officer."

She smiled. "Mr. Carolina."

"Have you lost weight?"

She laughed. "People always say that the first time they see me out of uniform. It's the Kevlar."

"Kevlar?"

"Body armor. Makes me look twenty pounds heavier."

"Does it weigh that much?"

"No, but it's pretty uncomfortable. Can we sit down?"

Carolina jumped. "Sure." He reached to pull out her chair,

then took his own. She watched him with an amused expression on her face.

"You look surprised."

Carolina hesitated. "I've never been out with a policewoman before."

"Want me to read you your rights?"

Before he could answer a waitress came to ask about drinks. They both ordered Pinot Grigio. The waitress disappeared.

"How'd you pick this place?" Carolina asked.

"I grew up in this town," Carla answered. "I know where the good food is."

A moment later the waitress returned with the wine and a plate of bruschetta, warm toasted garlic bread piled high with white beans, chopped peppers, and tomatoes.

"Quite a piece you had tonight," Carla said. "Nice work getting the scoop on the source of the dynamite."

"Thanks." Carolina sipped his wine.

"Did that come from ATF?"

Carolina smiled. "You know better than to ask that."

"Worth a shot," Carla answered. "They don't share anything with me."

"No? Why not?"

"Being an Environmental Police officer doesn't help. We're not exactly viewed with respect by some of your more old-fashioned police types. Then there's the woman thing."

"Kind of sexist, are they?"

Carla did not respond, and that itself was an answer.

"You mentioned some business on the telephone," Carolina said, taking a piece of the bruschetta.

"Yes. I saw your piece on the explosion tonight."

Carolina nodded. "Strange, isn't it?"

"What did you think of the description of the guy with the clams?"

Carolina looked at her, wondering for a moment what she was driving at. When the answer hit him, he swallowed hard.

"That guy in the quahog skiff."

Carla smiled and sipped her wine.

"I'll be damned."

"And I'd bet," she said, "that those two guys in the speedboat were the ones hassling him at the clam shack."

Carolina sipped from his glass, enjoying the feel of the pale, dry liquid that burned and cooled his throat at the same time.

"Do you have any idea who the two guys might be?"

Carla shook her head. "Just two guys in a fast boat."

"Well," Carolina said, "I may be able to help you there."

He told her about seeing the cigarette boat in Westerly, and how it was registered to Thelma Pitts. Carla listened to him describe the visit to Whipple Realty, and the stationery that referred to "Gaspee Gallery."

"Sounds pretty strange," Carla agreed. "But we still don't know what they were doing with Mitty."

"Mitty?"

"If I'm right," Carla said, "that's who our friend with the dynamite is."

"You know him?" Carolina said.

Carla ran a tanned finger across the edge of her glass. "I've never really met him," she said, "but I've heard of him. He's a renegade quahogger. Been around for years. Drives a little gray clam boat with a couple of big engines, and rakes the northern part of the bay."

"Is this for the record?"

"Not if you want me to keep talking to you, it isn't."

Carolina looked in her eyes, then back to the finger tracing the lip of the glass. He liked the way it moved, slowly, without a sound.

"I guess I have a dilemma," he said.

"What's that?"

"You just gave me some great information, but I can't use it."

"Not yet," Carla said. "But you know more now than any other reporter."

The waitress appeared again, this time with dinner. Fettucine carbonara, and rigatoni tossed with olives, red peppers, and fresh parmesan that had been scraped into long, slender threads, instead of being grated.

"I have never been anywhere," Carolina said, "where there were so many great restaurants."

Carla nodded. "When I was a little girl," she said, "my parents used to say that good food was part of a good life."

"I've been meaning to ask you," Carolina said.

"Ask me what?"

"How a girl from Johnston, with a history major from Brown, winds up as an Environmental Police officer."

"Well," Carla said, "I like the bay, and I like boats."

"You like being a cop?"

"Yes, I do," she said. "Though I'm not sure I want to do it forever."

"Why not?"

"It wears on you. People treat you differently. You're not Carla Tattaglia anymore, you're the woman with the gun and the badge. Even if"—she smiled wistfully—"even if it's just the Environmental Police." She looked at him. "You know what I mean, don't you?"

"Not exactly," Carolina said. "But I've heard other police officers say the same things."

"There's a lot of stress to it. Pressure. And you kind of have to put it away when you work."

"What else would you like to do?"

"You really want to know?"

"Sure."

"Maybe own my own restaurant."

"Is that right?"

"It takes some capital," Carla said, "and a lot of hard work. But I've never been afraid of that."

"Where would you want to do it?"

"Someplace in Providence, or maybe down by the water somewhere. It's hard to say. Why did you become a reporter?"

"I liked digging around. Questioning authority."

"You still like it?"

"Sometimes. Your perspective changes. I spent some time away from the business. Then I came back again."

"What did you do when you were away?"

"I had a sailboat. I took it to Tahiti."

"What was it like?"

"It was everything I thought it would be. Very challenging. Invigorating."

"What's the hardest part?"

"Being alone," Carolina said. "You only have yourself to depend on, and that's hard sometimes. But it's also the best thing."

"I like that," Carla said. "So where are you from?"

"I grew up in Iowa."

"Des Moines? Cedar Rapids?"

"Dubuque," Carolina said. "Right on the Mississippi."

"What got you so interested in sailing?"

"I liked watching the towboats," he said. "It looked like you could use them to go anywhere. When I left television a few years back, I bought an old boat, worked on it, and took off." He realized how she'd turned things around, that she was asking the questions now. But he didn't mind it. Carla Tattaglia made him feel comfortable. Very comfortable.

"So why did you leave television?"

"I didn't exactly have a choice," he said.

"You got fired?"

Carolina nodded, and drank.

"I guess that happens a lot in your business. What happened?"

"I did a story about my station's anchorman. He liked children."

"So?"

"He liked them a little too much."

"You mean—?"

"Yeah," Carolina said. "That's what I mean. The station didn't like what I did. I didn't like what the station did. They showed me the door. But I probably would have quit anyway."

Carla leaned over and brushed back a strand of her black, shiny hair. Carolina could smell the soap she'd used. She caught the look on his face and smiled.

"Why'd you get back into journalism again?"

"The money was better. And basically, it's the only thing I know how to do to make a living."

"Why here?"

"That's complicated," he said, and decided it would not be good to share everything just then. "One reason is I decided you can't just travel forever. Sooner or later, you have to get somewhere, and see if you like it. I've spent a lot of time traveling, a lot of time trying to find the perfect place to be."

"Have you found it?"

"This is an interesting state, Rhode Island," he said. "Wonderful history. All these restaurants. And the news stories, well . . ." He smiled.

Carla smiled back. "You didn't answer my question."

The verbal fencing between them had changed the mood, but not in an unpleasant way. It was almost as if the words, the looks they'd exchanged, had turned up some invisible thermostat.

"Let's just say," he told her, "that I like it here a lot. And I'd like to spend more time getting acquainted."

Carla didn't answer. But then, she didn't have to.

"How are we doing over here?" the waitress asked. They had consumed all of the pasta.

"It was great," Carolina said. "I'm stuffed."

The waitress grinned as she cleared the plates. These two, she thought, were definitely connecting.

Carla and Michael talked some more over coffee. He kept watching her hands and the way they moved. When the waitress brought the check they both reached for it.

"I asked you," Carla said.

"So? The state can't be paying you that well."

"I do just fine," she said, but finally gave in. "Thank you."

"What do we do now?" he said, not looking at her.

"I don't have any plans," Carla said.

They were both looking at each other now, each one wondering what the other was thinking, still trying to read expressions, gestures. The waitress came back with change, and Carolina left a healthy tip. They walked out of the restaurant together.

"You live around here?" Carolina asked.

"Not anymore," Carla said. "I just like the food."

Carolina said nothing for a moment.

"I have a house," Carla said, "a little one, down by Edgewood."

"Nice area," Carolina said. "Is it for sale?"

"No." Then, remembering what he'd said about Whipple Realty, she laughed.

"Do you want me to follow you?" he asked quietly.

Carla pulled her keys from a purse. "I hoped that you would," she said.

13

The room was airy, with big windows that opened toward the water. A three-quarter moon hung in the sky, and they could see each other in the dim light. Even though the night was warm, they were comfortable.

"That realtor was right," Carolina said.

"About what?"

"You really do get the breeze down here."

Carla smiled. With her left hand she traced a line along his chest. Down, then back again.

"Michael," she said.

"Yes."

"You're not a simple man."

"I'm not?"

"No. You're very unusual."

"Really?"

"Did I offend you?"

"No," he said. She slid closer to him.

"I hope I didn't upset you," Carla said.

"Why do you say that?"

"You just seem like—I don't know. My father, he used to get kind of quiet, distant sometimes. When he had something on his mind, you could almost feel it, even though he never said anything. And I kind of sense the same thing from you."

He stared into the darkness for a moment. "Were you close to your father?"

"Yes. He died last year. Are you close to your father?"

"Not exactly."

"Why not?"

Carolina realized then what Carla had sensed. He could not escape the images of the casino, and the memories those images stirred. "When I was growing up," he said, "my father used to gamble a lot. We lived across the river from a couple of casinos. Nothing big, just a couple of hole-in-the-wall places where people would go to throw away money. And my father got hooked. He couldn't stop shooting craps, or playing cards. He always had to have a bet down.

"It used to drive my mother crazy. He had a good job in one of the factories, and a beautiful wife, and—"

"And he had you," Carla offered.

"I guess," Carolina said. "But it wasn't enough. I can still remember one night when a sheriff came to the house, with a couple of movers. They took a television away that my father bought for us on some installment plan. Then a few weeks later the sheriff came back with an eviction notice. They moved all the furniture out of the house, right into the street. For all the neighbors to see. My mother kept holding on to this bag that had her clothes in it, and telling me to stop playing while we waited for one of my uncles to come get our things with his truck. There were all these people looking out the windows at us, and she just stood there, holding that bag, pretending they weren't looking at us, and telling me not to play."

"Where was your father?"

"Across the river, in one of those cheap casinos."

It was quiet then. In the distance they could hear the low, throaty sound of a ship's horn on a freighter, making its way toward the terminals in Providence.

"Do you know where your father is now?" Carla asked.

"He's still in Dubuque. Haven't seen him in years," Carolina said. "Not since my mother died."

"You should let the memories go," Carla said.

Carolina touched her hair, then kissed her. "Easier said than done."

118

She met them by the speedboat on the pier. The two of them looked rumpled, sweaty, and tired. They stood around looking at the checks in the wood pilings, scuffing their basketball shoes.

The woman looked them over, but offered no greeting. She reached into a small handbag and lit a cigarette. Despite the heat, she absently folded her arms close.

"Jimmy wanted me to talk to you."

"We know we fucked up," one of the men said. His name was Paulie, and he had soot on his sweatsuit and across his forehead.

"Don't worry about it," the woman said. "I got Jimmy under control."

"We tried," the other one said. His name was Liberato, but everyone called him Libby. "That fuckin' clamdigger's runnin' around with dynamite."

"I saw the news," the woman said sympathetically. "He's crazy."

"What were we gonna do?" Paulie asked.

The lady shrugged. "Don't worry about it. I think there's another way of dealing with this."

She reached for the bow line on the boat. Libby grabbed the stern line while Paulie fired the engine. In a minute the boat was easing into the narrow channel. In five minutes they were roaring across Block Island Sound.

"We headin' back up the bay? Go for that guy again?" Paulie called.

"Not yet," the woman shouted back. She watched Libby trying to wipe soot from the top of his jogging suit. He licked his palm and wiped the fabric. It made the stain worse.

"I gotta tell you guys," the lady screamed, "this wasn't that hard a job."

"Easy for you to say," Paulie shouted back. "You try bringing somebody in, he's got dynamite in his hand."

The woman gestured for him to bring the throttle back, and Paulie did, until the boat was idling in the water. Block Island

Sound was well lit from the three-quarter moon. Off to the northeast they could see the winking lights of Newport. But there were no boats in sight.

"What are we doing?" Paulie asked.

"Yeah, what are we doing?" Libby echoed. Paulie was the leader of the two men, the woman could see.

"Before we head in," the woman said, "I want to discuss a game plan. Jimmy wants this guy found, and we have to find him."

"I didn't know you was gonna help," Paulie said.

"Well, I am," the woman said. She looked at the bulge on Paulie's waist. "Hey, is that your piece?"

"Yeah."

The woman stopped clutching at herself. "Can I see it?"

The man named Paulie hesitated, but only for a second. She was a broad, sure, but Jimmy had sent her, right?

"Wow," the woman said, handling the piece. "What's this called again?"

".38. Jesus," Paulie said, shaking his head. Libby watched them, giggling.

"Sorry, guys," the lady said. "I know I sound stupid. I just don't know that much about guns."

The woman held the gun pointed toward the boat's deck. "Yeah, I don't know much about guns. Or about boats. What kind of engine does this thing have?"

"Inboard," Paulie said. "Four hundred horsepower. Ain't we gonna do something about this guy? That's what Jimmy sent you for, right?"

"Yeah, we're gonna do something," the lady said. "Where's the exhaust on this thing?"

"From the back, Jesus," Paulie said.

The woman looked at Libby, who was still giggling. "Can you show me?"

Libby looked at Paulie, who nodded his head in disgust. Libby picked himself up and moved to the back of the cigarette's cockpit, pointing over the side.

"I can't see it," the lady said. She stepped over next to him.

"It's right there," Libby said.

"Oh, there it is," the woman said. "Thanks for showing me."

Then she shot him in the head.

The force drove Libby off the boat and into the water. He lay there, suspended for a moment, then slipped into the black. The boat rocked gently, and the woman turned toward Paulie.

"Holy fuck," Paulie said.

"Now let's talk about my idea." The woman was quite calm.

"You're a complete moron, and it's only by whim that you're still alive. Jimmy said I could do you both. Understand?"

Paulie nodded.

"Now we are going to find this guy and we are going to find out what he was doing in Stillhouse Cove. And you are not going to screw this up any further than you have. Right?"

Paulie nodded again.

"Good."

The woman expertly opened the cylinder of the .38 and checked the load.

"I'll hold on to this for a while. If you fuck up again, I may need it." The woman tucked the gun into her purse and got another smoke. She lit up and drew a lungful of smoke.

"What are you looking at?" she snapped at the man, then drew her arms across her chest. "You think I want to spend the night out here with you? Start this thing up and take me home."

Paulie revved the engine and headed the boat back toward Westerly. It had been a terrifying experience, finding out the little clammer had live explosives, then riding out here with Libby. Worse, he'd been stupid enough to hand his piece over to the lady, and he was very nearly dead as a result. He looked back at her, sitting on one of the vinyl seats, smoking and shivering.

Still, he thought, she was one hell of a woman.

14

S o nice to see you at work on time," Shirley said.

"Good morning to you, too," Carolina said.

"You look happy."

"I'm fine, thank you. You need me for a story today?"

The news director's eyebrows arched in surprise. "You don't have anything to work on?"

"I have a lot to work on," he said. "I'm just trying to help."

"This isn't like you," Shirley said. "You're so—pleasant."

Carolina's neutral expression did not change.

"I don't think we need you for anything right now," Shirley said. "Have you had any luck figuring out what that Gaspee Gallery thing is all about?"

"No," Carolina said. "But I'm not ready to quit."

Shirley kept looking at him, trying to figure out what was different. Carolina didn't say a word.

"Let me know how it's going," Shirley said. Carolina nodded and she walked away.

He waited until she slipped back into her office, then picked up the phone. A sleepy voice answered.

"Did I wake you?" he asked.

"No," Carla said. "I was just lying here, thinking about what a nice time I had last night."

"Glad you feel that way," he said. He tried to imagine what she looked like then, in the big airy bedroom of her Edgewood house.

"And you?"

"I'm fine."

"What are you working on today?" Carla asked.

"Some of the stuff we were talking about last night. I was wondering if I could ask you a favor."

"Depends on what it is," Carla said.

"Could you run an NCIC check on Thelma Pitts?" The term referred to the National Crime Information Center's data bank, which held information on virtually every known criminal in the United States.

Carla hesitated. "I know you're looking for help, Michael, but ATF's got an active investigation going."

"So?"

"So, I don't want to step on their toes. Besides, they've already indicated they're not interested in my help."

Carolina thought for a minute. "Remember what I mentioned about the boat? The big speedboat?"

"The one we saw on the bay that night? What about it?"

"Well, your records people say the boat's registered to Thelma Pitts."

"But we don't even know it's the same boat. It could be. But we never saw the name that night. You're guessing that the boat you saw in Westerly is the same one we saw that night."

Carolina knew she was correct.

"But I have to admit," Carla said, "it was a good guess."

"Can you get in a lot of trouble over this?" Carolina asked.

"Using NCIC for a reporter? What do you think?"

"Don't worry about it," he said.

"Michael, I didn't say I wouldn't do it. But—"

"But what?"

"I don't want to be bending the rules just because I slept with you."

Carolina tapped a pen on his desk quietly, drumming a rhythm without realizing it.

"That's not the only reason I called," he said, finally.

"No?" Carla said, doubtful.

"Can we get together later?" he asked.

"I have to work tonight," she said.

"Okay," he said.

"But maybe."

They hung up. Carolina stopped drumming the pen. He was still for a moment, trying to figure out what the phone call was really all about.

The day was not as warm as the one before, and Carolina was grateful. He drove the unmarked station car into South Providence, then Edgewood, and parked half a block from the entrance of Whipple Realty. With the motor and air-conditioning off the temperature inside quickly rose to over one hundred. He left the windows down, and turned the engine over every few minutes, but the relief was fleeting.

The woman who called herself Molly Whipple had answered her phone that morning before he left the station, so he knew she was at work. He sat in the car, sweating and praying that she would come out to show someone a house.

Carolina thought about Carla and the night before. The dinner and the conversation, and what followed. Carla was an intelligent, thoughtful woman. Despite her work, she struck him as more sensitive than Marie, but perhaps a bit less confident. Marie. He wondered what she was doing, perhaps sitting in her air-conditioned law office or conducting a trial somewhere. Performance artists, finger paints, and juggled cucumbers.

"Shit," Carolina said out loud. He looked around to see if anyone had heard him. Cars continued to drive by, but otherwise the street was empty.

And then the man walked into Whipple Realty.

He had white hair, Carolina could see. White hair and a slightly reddened face. He looked vaguely familiar, but Carolina could not remember from where.

The man was inside the office for less than five minutes when the door opened and he came out again, this time with Molly Whipple in tow. The two of them set off down the street, stopping next to an unremarkable blue Chevrolet. The man climbed into the driver's seat, started up, and quickly slipped into traffic.

Carolina started his engine, pulled out, and nearly collided with an oncoming Bronco. The other driver screeched to a halt, then cursed loud enough for Carolina to hear.

"Nice to see you," Carolina mouthed, stepping on the gas. The near accident had allowed the blue Chevy to move ahead another block, and at least five cars separated it from Carolina. A stoplight slowed him down again, and he could see the car draw even farther ahead, then turn off to the right. Carolina cursed. The Chevy was gone.

The stoplight turned green and he roared up the street, dodging cars and changing lanes, trying to find a way to catch up. He took the same right that the Chevy had, and barreled down the street, looking everywhere for a sign of the car. There was none.

It was an old residential neighborhood. Carolina looked for Whipple Realty signs and saw none. He reached the end of the street and saw he had a choice. There was an entrance to I-95, one going north, the other south. Which way would they go, he wondered to himself. There were no hints as to which was the right choice.

Carolina chose north. He pulled toward the on-ramp, rounding a curve, accelerating as the road straightened. The traffic was moderately heavy, with lots of commercial vehicles taking care of daily business. Carolina looked ahead for any sign of the blue Chevy, but saw nothing. He sped up and pulled into the far left lane, speeding up to the sixty-five as he approached the split for I-195, the road that led east to Cape Cod. He looked for an instant at the digital clock on the station car's dash: 11:58.

The next road sign warned it was half a mile to the 195 split. Carolina slipped back into a middle lane, still undecided as to which road to take. This is stupid, he told himself. They probably already took another exit.

If the red semi had not stomped on his brakes and shifted left he would not have seen it. Carolina stepped on his own brakes, checked the mirror, and shifted again to the far right lane. He looked ahead, and there was the blue Chevrolet, taking the lane for I95.

"Damn," he said to himself.

He slowed down again, keeping his eye on the car as it passed the downtown Providence exit, then slowed down. The next exit came up fast. Wickenden Street. The driver's brake lights came on, but he did not use his turn signal while he left the highway. Carolina slowed as much as he could, hoping for another car to pass him and take the exit for Wickenden Street. It seemed to take forever, but finally, a gray Lexus pulled onto the ramp. Carolina sped up suddenly, wondering how private investigators ever managed to tail people for extended periods of time.

The Chevrolet drove up Wickenden and turned left. Carolina maintained a respectable distance. He followed for another mile, until the car pulled to the side of the road and parked. Carolina drove past, watching as the man and Molly Whipple got out. From the rearview he could see them crossing the street.

He circled the block and parked, then ran back to the spot where he'd last seen the two of them. They were just turning into a parking lot, and disappeared again. Carolina trotted up the street once more, and turned just in time to see the couple approaching the entrance to a restaurant called Adesso. Lunchtime. The woman named Molly Whipple, cigarette in hand, grabbed the door. The man did a half turn, and took the door from her, and Carolina looked at him again. Then the woman was inside, the man following behind her.

And now Carolina remembered him.

He decided not to follow. A single person eating in a restaurant nearly always stands out, and he feared the woman would recognize him. Besides, lunch in an upscale restaurant was bound to take an hour. Instead, Carolina walked toward Thayer Street, looking for a pay phone.

"Can you get me a photographer and a surveillance van?" he asked when Shirley got on the phone.

"What have you got?"

"I don't know yet," Carolina said, "but I figured you'd kill me if I didn't try to get a shot of our realtor friend having lunch with a mobster."

15

Will you look at that," Shirley said, watching the beta tape roll. The video was slightly grainy, having been shot through the tinted back door of an unmarked van. Two figures were seen emerging from the parking lot of Adesso, strolling down the sidewalk. The pair walked past the van, an older man with his hands in his pockets, and Whipple, smoking away.

"So that's Jimmy Flannery?"

"The one and only," Carolina said.

"What are they talking about?"

The fact was that neither appeared to be saying much, and the video was not clear enough to show lips moving. Carolina and Shirley watched in silence as the man and the woman walked out of frame, then listened to the rumble and hiss of Earl struggling to reposition his camera to get one more shot of them walking toward their car out of the van's front window. When the camera settled, Flannery was already reaching for the front door of his car. He looked across at Whipple, her back now to the camera. She said something that made him scowl and shake his head. Then the couple ducked inside the vehicle and drove off.

"Interesting stuff," Shirley said. "But we still don't know what it means."

"I don't think they know each other by accident," Carolina said.

"So what's the connection?"

He had no answer.

"For all we know," Shirley said, "he wants to buy a house."

"You don't believe that," Carolina said.

"No, I don't. But we need more than this to get a story out of it. Which reminds me."

"Of what?"

"That I'm shorthanded this weekend. Can you work a day shift for me on Saturday?"

He'd spent a day trailing Molly Whipple, and found she had a dangerous and powerful friend. He'd even grabbed a piece of video that might prove useful later, if he ever figured out what was going on with Whipple and Stillhouse Cove and the man called Mitty Navel. But now Shirley was calling in a favor.

"Sure," Carolina said. "I don't have any plans."

"Good," she said.

A page from the station's receptionist announced that Carolina had a visitor.

"You expecting someone?" Shirley asked.

"No," Carolina said.

"When you're finished, come see me again. I'll tell you what you're covering Saturday."

Sally Generous was holding an armload of papers when Carolina walked into the station lobby.

"You remember me, Mr. Carolina?"

"How could I forget?"

Her hair was pulled back in a tight bun, and she reached up with one hand to wipe away a strand that had somehow slipped away.

"I had some information I thought might interest you."

He pointed to a couch and she sat down, practically spilling the papers onto the couch next to her. Generous started to riffle through the papers, absently bouncing a hairy leg.

"What kind of information?" Carolina asked.

Finding what she was looking for, Sally handed him a typed report. The document was authored by a marine biologist from Woods Hole, Massachusetts. It was called "Salt Water Farms: Aquaculture Opportunities in Narragansett Bay."

"This is what Save the Chowder is all about," Sally said. "We're trying to take back the waters of the bay, to make them safe for the clammers and oystermen."

"And the people who eat their catch?"

Sally looked perplexed for a moment. "Of course," she said. "That's what I meant."

Carolina looked at the materials for a moment. Sally watched him nervously.

"Why do you want me to read these?" Carolina asked.

Sally bounced her leg even harder. "Because I think we got off to a bad start," she said. "And because of the float."

"The what?"

"You know, the float." She looked at him for a moment, perplexed. "Are you teasing me?" she asked.

"I'm sorry," Carolina said, "but I haven't got a clue what you're talking about."

"Aren't you the reporter covering the *Gaspee* Days parade?"

"Not to my knowledge." Now Carolina looked perplexed.

"Well, I spoke to Shirley Templeton about it. I guess she'll fill you in. Anyway, you should read those reports. It explains why preservation of the bay is so important."

Sally Generous seemed so eager, so driven, so . . . intense. She reminded Carolina of a high school cheerleader who'd been brainwashed by some radical faction of the Sierra Club.

"So is this a nonprofit group?" Carolina asked.

Sally nodded vigorously. "Absolutely. We're totally nonprofit, and donations are tax deductible. And our workers are all volunteers."

"How long have you been with the organization?"

Generous thought for a moment. "It'll be two years in August. I'm the founder, actually."

"How do you support yourself?"

Generous hesitated. "That's kind of personal."

"Sorry." Carolina shrugged.

"I have a trust fund," Sally blurted. "And I'm not going to be with Save the Chowder forever, you know."

"What are you going to do?"

She looked at him for a minute. Carolina had the impression she was trying to be coy.

"I'm building a track record," she said, finally.

"For what?"

"For my future."

"I don't know what you're talking about," he said, then stopped. He finally understood.

"You're planning to run for office?"

"I never said that," Sally said. She looked nervous again, afraid she'd said too much.

"What," Carolina said, "Congress? General Assembly?"

Sally did not respond, but the look on her face was enough. She rose, clutching more reports. "I've got to go."

"Why, just when we're getting to know each other?"

"You're teasing me."

"A little. Nothing serious."

Sally Generous turned to look at him as she stood at the station door.

"This was all off the record, right?"

"Sure," Carolina said. "We were just talking."

He walked back to the newsroom, glancing over the papers she had left. They were more than an inch thick, filled with discussion of pollution levels, shellfish contamination, and a history of oyster and clam harvesting in New England. He set them down at his desk, and saw Shirley beckoning.

"I wanted to talk to you about your assignment this weekend."

"What's this about a parade?" Carolina asked.

Shirley paused. "The Gaspee Days parade is a Rhode Island tradition. Channel Three is co-sponsoring a float."

"Co-sponsoring?" Then it dawned on him. "Oh no."

"Oh yes," Shirley said. "We're sponsoring the float with Save the Chowder."

"You're ordering me to shill for the station?"

"Not at all," Shirley said. "The GM is ordering you to shill for the station. I'm just the messenger."

Promoting a station's "image" was one of the prices to be paid for working in the television news business. Viewers always wanted to be close to the so-called "celebrities" who brought death, disaster, weather, and sports to them each evening. Channel Three was no exception. Some reporters and anchors loved the opportunity to promote the station: it often meant free food and a chance to be admired by the public. Carolina hated it.

"I really don't want to ride on a float, Shirl."

"I knew you were going to say that," Shirley said. "You don't have to."

"Thank you."

"But you do have to work the float into your story about the parade."

Carolina pursed his lips and considered possible counterarguments.

"I know you don't like this," Shirley said, "but station promotion is a fact of life in this industry."

"Uh-huh," Carolina said.

"Besides, Save the Chowder is a good cause."

"Right."

Shirley sighed. "Sally Generous should be dropping off some literature about aquaculture for you to read."

"She already has."

"Good," Shirley said. "That gives you something to do."

"So," Carolina said, "is one of our anchors riding on the float?"

"No," Shirley said. "Chelsea is."

Chelsea Alvarez was Channel Three's new morning weather personality, a twenty-five-year-old Cuban-American beauty who freely explained to anyone who would listen that she despised Providence and couldn't wait for a job to become available in her hometown of Miami.

"Marvelous," Carolina said.

"I'm so glad that you're handling this in a professional manner," Shirley said. "I have great confidence that your story will be spectacular."

Carolina ate a solitary TV dinner in his apartment, then walked down to Thayer Street. It was just starting to get dark, and the sidewalks were filled with panhandlers and the high school kids who used the street as an outdoor mall in the summer. The panhandlers wore coats and leather jackets because they had nowhere else to keep them. The kids sported a variety of fluorescent hairstyles and kept pieces of steel in their noses and ears. Carolina felt slightly out of place.

He looked through some jazz records in one of the stores, and thought about picking up a Miles Davis CD until he remembered he had not yet purchased a CD player for the apartment. He examined the books at Brown and College Hill, but there was nothing that piqued his interest.

He started walking back up Thayer Street just as the Avon theater was letting out the crowd from the early show, some sort of Dutch animation festival that had attracted a rather eclectic audience. Just as he was nearing the door he saw Marie walking out the door. The cucumber-juggling performance artist was not with her. Instead, she was accompanied by a rail-thin giant with brown greasy hair and a goatee. The man was gesturing and chatting excitedly, apparently about the performance the two had just seen. Marie seemed to hang on every word.

Carolina quickly turned his head and studied the poster that listed coming attractions. There was nothing that interested him. If that's exotic, I can do without it, he thought to himself. When he turned his head again, Marie and her new friend had disappeared.

He walked home. The apartment was dark, warm, stifling. He turned on a wall unit air conditioner, let the freon wash over him, and tried not to think about calling Carla Tattaglia.

The phone rang.

"Hello."

"Hi," Carla said.

"Hi." Carolina smiled.

"Where have you been?" Carla asked.

"Out for a walk on Thayer Street."

"How was it?"

"Solitary," Carolina said. "What have you been doing?"

"Working. Kind of a quiet day," she said. "I was wondering if you were going to call."

"I thought about it," Carolina said. "But after this morning, I thought you needed—you know—"

"Space?"

Carolina's smile changed to a grimace. "I guess," he said.

"Well," Carla said. "I'm sorry if I put you off."

"Not a problem," Carolina said.

"It's been a while since I've seen anyone," Carla said. "I just want to be careful."

"Okay."

Neither one said anything for a moment.

"I'm glad you called," Carolina said.

"So am I," Carla said. "So why is this so hard?"

"Because we don't know each other that well."

Carla laughed a little. "You're right. Don't you hate that? It would be so much easier if we could all carry some kind of sign around with us to see if we connect."

"Like litmus paper?" Carolina asked.

"Exactly."

Now it was getting easier. With just a few words, they both felt the attraction again. Even the silence felt more comfortable.

"So," Carla said, "What are you doing?"

"Cooling off," he said. "This is tough for me, living in the city."

"You're more used to boats?"

"Yeah. I feel a little trapped."

"Well," Carla said. "I don't live on a boat, but you know what the realtors here say?"

"What's that?"

"We do get the breeze in Edgewood."

"I hate realtors," Carolina said. "But I like the breeze."

"Never met a sailor who didn't."

"So this is an invitation?"

"It is," Carla said.

"I see. What can I bring?"

"Bottle of wine would be nice."

"Check."

"Don't bother with pajamas," Carla said. "You won't be needing them."

*S*aturday's weather was the same as it had been all week, but the people in Edgewood and Pawtuxet Cove had no time to care. Gaspee Days came just once a year, in June, and the parade committee intended for this to be the best parade ever.

There were nearly a dozen high school bands from Cranston and Warwick, Pawtucket and East Providence, and one from a Catholic high school in Fall River. They were joined by a group of American Legion members from a post in North Kingstown, and a fife and drum outfit dressed in tricorn hats and knee breeches. A group of Civil War reenactors, seeking any excuse for a little marching, tugged at their wool jackets and kepis, while a college ROTC color guard from the University of Rhode Island tried not to scratch at the harnesses that held their flags firmly against their respective crotches.

They all began to line up not long after dawn, tuning instruments, twirling batons, checking buttons on coats, and adjusting hats. A group of Shriners checked the engine oil of a squadron of go-carts, then turned to adjusting each other's fezzes. Actors dressed as Abraham Whipple and his gang of shipburners gathered to do one final rehearsal of a skit, while a group of junior high school boys buffed a set of Cadillacs that would hold the grand marshal and the herd of politicians that inevitably appeared in an election year.

By nine A.M., the temperature had already pushed into the high eighties. The band members started developing large sweat spots underneath their arms. A few scuffles broke out around the

Del's Frozen Lemonade vendors, who did outstanding business as people tried to get something cool to drink.

"I chust *hate* this weather," Chelsea Alvarez moaned.

She fanned herself with a copy of the Providence *Herald* as she walked with Carolina and Earl. The traffic forced them to abandon their van half a mile from the parade's staging area and the Save the Chowder float.

"You should be used to it, being from Miami," Earl huffed, lugging his camera. Carolina carried the photographer's tripod and a bag of spare batteries and tapes. Chelsea did not offer to assist.

"In Mi-jami we have AC for days like thees." On air, Chelsea had excellent diction, the product of ten thousand dollars' worth of lessons paid for by her father, South Florida's first Cuban chiropractor. But under stress, she lapsed into an accent entirely foreign to Rhode Island viewers. Walking to a parade site evidently qualified as a stressful event.

"Isn't it hot during the Orange Bowl parade?" Carolina asked.

"That's in the weenter." Chelsea threw him a withering glance. "Eet's nice in the weenter." She had no patience for those who knew little of South Florida.

Earl stopped for a moment to ease the strap that held his camera off his shoulder. He removed a Red Sox baseball cap and wiped his brow.

"You okay?" Carolina asked.

"Fine," he said. "What are we looking for?"

Just then they saw it, sitting in a line of parade floats, balanced precariously on top of a small, sea-green pickup truck.

"Whoa," Earl said.

"What's that?" Chelsea asked.

Carolina simply gaped. It was a mass of gray papier-mâché, the outsides curved and lined with touches of white and flecks of gold. The insides had a burst of orange and red, muted by more gray, all of it in lines from one edge to the other.

Sally Generous appeared, wearing shorts and a halter top. She waved, exposing a brown, unshaved pit.

"How are you?" she asked. "Like the float?"

"That," Carolina said, "is amazing."

"What is it?" Chelsea asked again.

Earl gulped. "That's the biggest fucking quahog I've ever seen."

"The biggest what?" Chelsea said, distaste showing in her voice.

"It's a clam, Chelsea," Carolina said. "It's the symbol of Save the Chowder."

"Don't you love it?" Sally said, walking over to stroke the papier-mâché shell. "It took us *weeks* to build it."

"And let me guess," Carolina said, "Chelsea gets to ride in it?"

Sally beamed. "There's a seat welded to the lower half of the shell." She stuck out a hand to Chelsea Alvarez.

"You must be the weather woman."

Chelsea gave a limp hand and mumbled softly in Spanish.

"She says she's thrilled to be here," Carolina said. "Can't wait for the parade to start."

"Want to do an interview now?" Sally asked.

"Why don't we grab some of the parade first," Carolina said. "We'll catch up with you later."

"Where are joo going?" Chelsea demanded. She was obviously distressed at being left with the giant clam and the woman from Save the Chowder.

Carolina smiled. "Got a story to do."

Mitty Navel was thirsty.

He was torturing himself, really, watching crowds of people pushing to grab cups of frozen lemonade frantically being spooned by vendors along the Pawtuxet Village parade route. Mitty remembered how his mother had once purchased a cup of the stuff to drink at a parade when he was a little boy, how cool and sweet it felt going down on a hot day.

He touched his pocket, knowing he had just two dollars and fifty cents to his name. He'd thrown away his clams; they were too rotten even for the seedier chowder and clam shacks of the West Bay. His truck was nearly out of gas. There would be no lemonade today.

He lugged a sack over his shoulder, down the street, through the growing swell of parade observers. The crowd parted easily, since Mitty had not had a bath in a week. He finally found his way to a Mobil station and asked to use a water fountain. The sweaty attendant held his nose and nodded. The water was tepid. Mitty took two slurps and worked his way back toward the crowd.

"What's that, Mommy?" a red-faced little boy asked his mother as the scruffy little quahogger shuffled past.

"Don't stay-uh, honey," the woman said, her eyes watering. Mitty heard, but ignored them. He kept moving.

The parade began on schedule, with a crash of drums and horns, mixing in with sirens from the local fire companies. The Gaspee Days celebration was under way.

Paulie liked parades, watched them on TV, and sometimes went to the St. Joseph's Day festival up on Federal Hill. But it was too damned hot. Too freakin' wet, he thought. On a day like this, a February blizzard looked good.

What he couldn't understand was how his partner could stay so cool. Literally. She wore jeans and a light blouse, carried a purse that held the .38, and smoked like a chimney. But there wasn't a drop of perspiration, not even a slight glow. The woman's eyes were masked by dark, round sunglasses, but she was absolutely calm.

"Youse want a drink?" he asked, hurrying to keep up with her.

"No," she said, not looking at him. "We've got work to do."

"I know, but it's hot, and I was thinkin'—"

"Don't strain yourself."

"I was thinkin' we could, you know, get some beers. When we finish."

The woman stopped walking for a minute. The crowd of parade watchers ignored them or walked past, looking for a better spot to see the show.

"Maybe you didn't understand me out on the boat."

"I undastood," Paulie said, hurt. "Business is business. I just figured, you know, when we find him—"

Paulie couldn't help it. There was something about a woman with a gun, a woman not afraid to use it, a woman who didn't— sweat . . . He suddenly wished he'd not worn boxers under his Bermuda shorts.

The woman who called herself Molly noticed.

"I see you brought your boy with you," she said.

Paulie blushed. For the first time, the woman laughed.

"My, and what a fine-looking fellow he is, too."

She started walking again. He looked around for a second, to see if anyone else had noticed. Then he ran to catch up with her.

"What are we doing here, again?" he asked.

The woman picked up her pace. She glanced at him once, a half smile on her face, and pulled out another cigarette.

"One of the clam-shack owners called Jimmy this morning. Said your friend the digger always comes to the parade. So we look for him."

"Okay." Paulie tried to sound more confident.

"Yeah. Then maybe, if you're a good boy, I'll go looking for Mr. Goodbar."

The Pawtuxet Rangers were in rare form, strutting down Narragansett Parkway to the rhythm of the drums and the twitter of fifes. The Rangers looked splendid, decked out in colonial-era uniforms, carrying muskets and waving madly to the crowd. They hauled a small cannon behind them and would stop occasionally to fire off a blank salute, all to the applause of the gathered spectators. A group of Shriners followed, led by an obese man clad in silk trousers. The Shriner engaged in a strange dance involving his ceremonial scimitar. He bobbed and whirled, thrusting the sword into the air, swinging it down again toward the pavement, spraying onlookers with his perspiration. His colleagues whizzed past in their go-carts. The crowd cheered again.

It made Mitty homesick. Mom always took him to the parade. Always made sure he got a chance to see the show.

He missed his mother, and longed for the chance to talk with someone, anyone, about the problems that had turned his life upside down. But Mom was long gone, buried in a Cranston cemetery, and there was no one else.

Despite the push of the crowd, people gave Mitty ample room, the smell of dead sea life and perspiration driving them back like an ax splitting wood. Mitty paid them no mind. He stared at the marchers, the floats, the sweaty Shriner with the sword and the go-carts.

Farther down the parade route came the sound of another band, an outfit of aging World War Two veterans moving slowly in the heat. Behind them the crowd cheered. Floats were making their way along the route, including the giant clam.

Mitty stared again. The sounds of the crowd diminished, then faded completely as the shell drew closer, heat shimmering off the pavement. He squinted, trying to drive the image away, but when he opened his eyes again the clam was just a few yards away. On a good day, with food in his belly and a lower amount of stress, Mitty might have laughed the thing off. But the clam was . . . moving. It kept coming. And . . . there was a *woman* inside.

"You rolling on this?" Carolina asked.

"Of course," Earl said, staring through his viewfinder. "This has to make the gag reel."

They had already taped the Shriners and the *Gaspee* reenactors, interviewed a parade organizer, shot a standup, and grabbed the obligatory sound bites from spectators. Now they were watching as the Save the Chowder float worked its way up toward the camera lens. Both were struggling to keep from laughing. This was because of Chelsea Alvarez. Perched inside the clam's jaws, she looked absolutely miserable, fanning herself with one hand and feebly attempting to wave with the other.

Station management, Carolina surmised, had undoubtedly intended to boost Channel Three's image by sending a "celebrity" to ride in the float. But the move backfired. Chelsea had only been working for the station for six weeks. As the third-rated station in town, that meant that hardly anyone knew who she was. With the intense heat, and the way the clam shell engulfed her, the first public appearance of Channel Three's new weather woman was a disaster.

"I can't believe that they'll run this," Earl said.

"They will," Carolina said. "It's a weekend. There's nothing else going on. The producer needs to fill up the hole."

"You're probably right," Earl said. "But it's still weird. She looks like she's being eaten alive."

Mitty Navel thought exactly the same thing.

The stifling heat proved too much. He was no longer at a parade. No longer watching the familiar images of his youth. The world was under attack. Narragansett Boulevard was besieged. Not by the British. By gargantuan, man-eating clams.

The woman was dying. He could see it in her face. She was in agony, being chewed by a monster quahog as it crushed a truck. The crowd stood by, wailing and yelling, waving and laughing. Mitty could hear none of it. The hallucination was so powerful, all he could see was the clam. And the girl.

Gotta do something, he thought. Gotta stop it.

He took a step forward. The people nearby paid no attention. They were watching the clam, and it was almost on them now. Larger than life. The girl inside was so dark, so tired, so beautiful. She turned to look at him, her face awash in pain.

He took another step. Gotta do something.

* * *

"I see him," Paulie said.

The woman turned her head. "Where?"

"Down there"—he pointed—"by that big fuggin' quahog."

"That bushy-headed little twerp?"

Paulie gave her a sheepish look. "That's the guy."

The woman who went by the name Molly Whipple watched Navel as he swayed back and forth. He was watching the clam float, paying no attention to anyone else around him.

"Can't move on him here," Paulie mumbled. "Too many people around."

Molly Whipple knew this, of course. She noticed, however, that the crowd gave the little clamdigger a wide berth. Being upwind of him, she had no idea why. Paulie noticed the satchel dangling from Mitty's shoulder.

"Think he's packin' more dynamite?" Paulie asked.

"How would I know?" Molly Whipple snapped.

Paulie looked slightly wounded. "Just trying to be helpful." Navel was still swaying, transfixed by the clam float. She watched as he took another step forward. He was now out of the crowd, a foot or two into the parade route. Still, no one came near him. Over one shoulder, she noticed, he carried a satchel.

"If he's carrying anything," she said, "it's in that bag."

"Yeah," Paulie said, delighted to agree with her.

"Okay, big guy," she said, starting to move closer to the clam float. "We get as close to him as we can."

"Okay."

"Stay away from the bag."

"And what else?"

"Just let me work."

Mitty was following the float as it crept along the boulevard. The crowd continued to move back as he passed. Chelsea noticed him. She waved, hoping it would pacify him and he would go away. But Mitty kept pace.

Every once in a while, Chelsea caught a whiff of the short man with the wild hair following the float. It was nauseating, but there was nothing to be done. Chelsea was more miserable than ever.

It all made sense now, Mitty thought. The woman was so beautiful, so petite, so *stoic* in her suffering. Her eyes had met his, and she had even waved, as the shellfish consumed her. She needs me, he thought. I can help her. I can do it. I can save her.

I gotta do something. Gotta.

"Jeez, you see that guy?" Earl laughed.

Carolina nodded. "I smell him, too."

The photographer rolled more tape. "Looks like he's in love."

The two of them laughed as they watched the man watching the clam float. Chelsea was now trying to ignore him, but it was no use.

"You get a picture of that guy?"

"Sure," Earl said. "The techs are gonna love this stuff."

Carolina noticed how much room the crowd was giving the man. Apparently there weren't any police around to move him back. Someone ought to move him out of there, he thought.

At the same moment a woman emerged from the crowd. A woman he knew. Molly Whipple. She was followed by a beefy man. The woman headed straight toward the bushy-haired fellow, though she appeared to be looking in another direction. In a moment she smacked into him.

17

M itty Navel crashed to the ground.

"Excuse me," the woman said, loudly, in case anyone was listening. "I didn't see you." She reached down to grab at the man's satchel, and as she did she lowered her voice. "Don't move, scumbag."

Mitty looked up. He'd never seen the woman before. Her face was tight, her eyes sharp. Over her shoulder peered another face. This one was familiar. From the clam shack. The goombah.

What are they doing here? Where's the clam? Where's the lady in the clam?

He could not hear the woman, though her mouth was moving, and her hand, close to his body, was poking at him. What were they saying?

The heat of the sun bore down on Mitty.

"Come on, dirtball," Paulie said, trying to help.

The little man looked up, but said nothing. Molly Whipple was getting angry. She tugged at the bag.

"Did you hear me?" she said. "I've got a gun in your ribs. Now get up and let's go before I blow you into the bay."

What do they want? He felt the woman pushing him, nudging him. Then a word or two began to seep through.

Go. Let's go.

The woman's face softened for a moment. He looked at her, so cool in the heat, telling him to go, go. The big man behind him,

145

opening his mouth, and then smiling at him. Then the woman again. I'm hot. I'm just so hot, and I must go.

Mama.

It was Mama looking at him, telling him to get up, that it was time to do some work, to go dig a bucket of clams. Go dig, and save that girl. That girl. Locked in the jaws of a quahog.

Yeah, Mom. Yeah.

Mitty was small, and days without food had left him weak. But there was something about an order from Mother.

The force of Mitty rising surprised Paulie and Molly Whipple. It knocked them back, and off balance, just enough for Mitty to swing free. The satchel went with him. The crowd that stood nearby let out a collective murmur, and Molly Whipple struggled to slide the .38 back under her blouse.

Mitty did not look back. He staggered off, toward the float. Toward the truck with the clam that was larger than life.

I gotta do it, his fried brain was telling him. I gotta save her. It's what my mother wants.

It was Chelsea Alvarez's worst nightmare.

The bushy-haired little man charged up onto the truck bed and into the clamshell.

"I save you," he said.

Chelsea let out a shriek. The crowd, unsure of what was happening, was quiet. Chelsea shrieked again as Mitty hefted her onto one shoulder.

"Save you," he said.

A little boy giggled, thinking it was part of the parade. Then another child, an eight-year-old girl, shouted.

"He's just like Quasimodo, Mommy. Like the bell ringer."

The mother was not so sure, but other children in the crowd agreed, as they watched the little quahogger climb down from the clam.

*　　*　　*

The driver of the truck was an old friend of the Generous family. He'd reluctantly donated his S-10 for the day because his mother insisted that Sally's "little chowder business" was a worthy cause.

"Isn't this great?" Sally asked from the passenger seat.

"Right," he said, wondering whether the papier-mâché clam would ruin the truck's paint job.

"The children love it," Sally said, watching the children shout and point.

"Adults don't seem so thrilled," the driver answered. The truck shook violently as Chelsea's scream was muffled by the truck's closed windows and air-conditioning.

"What's she doing up there?" the driver asked.

The truck shook again. Sally Generous beamed. "She must be dancing. It's probably a Latin thing."

Mitty left the clam truck, leaping a full three feet back to the pavement. Chelsea screamed again, mumbled words in Spanish, her voice filled with panic.

"Look what he's doing," Paulie said.

Molly Whipple was already looking. But there were too many people, too many eyes, all of them focused on the squat man and the screaming weather girl.

Finally a man stepped from the crowd. He walked quickly toward Mitty, now staggering down the street.

"Hey, buddy," he said. "Let her go."

Paulie and Molly Whipple could not hear his words. But they saw the little man's hands go diving into his satchel and emerge with a stick. So did everyone else within fifty feet, including Chelsea, who promptly fainted. Mitty let her slip to the ground.

The man put his hands up and quickly backed away. Mitty was not reassured. In a moment the lighter was out and flickering. The crowd, already uneasy, panicked. Dozens of people were screaming, pulling children, falling down, running into one another. Then the stick of dynamite was in the air, lobbed underhand toward the man who had intervened, and was now running full speed past the truck.

"Hit the deck!" Paulie said, and fell on top of Molly Whipple.

"Get down!" Carolina said, pulling Earl toward the pavement. The photographer did not fight him. But in one of the more brilliant moves of his journalistic career, Earl had the presence of mind to keep rolling.

The epicenter of the blast was just to the left rear of the S-10. It lifted the truck nearly ten feet off the ground and drove it at least fifteen feet forward before it came to rest, with a metallic crunching sound, on the passenger side.

The giant clam fared no better. It was launched another fifty feet into the air before disintegrating into shards and particles of papier-mâché and chicken wire. A few of the pieces landed on parade spectators. A few suffered cuts or bruises, but most were unhurt.

The most serious injury was to Sally Generous, who suffered a slight concussion and a simple fracture to her right arm. The driver intermittently bemoaned the loss of his truck and cursed Sally for getting him into this mess. Goddammit, he swore, he never should have listened to his mother, good causes be damned, if he ever saw another clam again as long as he lived it would be too soon, and "Sally, your organization's goddamned insurance premiums better be paid up because I ain't payin' to fix my own truck. Fuckin' A, you can count on that."

In the madness and mayhem that followed the explosion, Mitty Navel and Chelsea evaporated. Paulie the goombah and Molly Whipple also disappeared.

18

Shirley Templeton's dismay over the kidnapping of Chelsea Alvarez was muted by the awesome sights recorded on Earl's video.

"Michael, this tape is incredible." The camera caught the full power of the detonation, complete with fire, smoke, and milling spectators.

"I mean, it's unbelievable. Are you all right?"

Carolina touched a bandage on his arm, where he'd been cut by a piece of chicken wire. Earl had been hit by the same piece, opening a small gash on the back of his neck.

"We're okay," Carolina said into the cell phone.

"Good. We're going to need you live every fifteen minutes for the next hour. Then we'll do a piece at six, and probably a special at six-thirty. Shit, we may get another Pickering Award for this—"

"What about Chelsea?"

Shirley took a sharp breath. "No one has seen her. I've got calls in to the Cranston police and Rhode Island State Police."

"You put a reporter on it?"

"We're trying to get someone in." Shirley sounded frustrated. "It's hard reaching anyone on the weekends."

"Maybe I should go."

"No! I mean—we need you to go live, to talk about the explosion." She hung up before he could think of a response.

It was cool inside the microwave van, with the air conditioner blasting to cool the transmitting equipment. The frozen air matted Carolina's shirt against his back and made it feel like a piece

149

of cellophane. It was a strange sensation, but it felt good after all the outdoor heat. He punched the PLAY button on the van's playback deck and watched the video roll once more. In a moment he could feel himself perspiring again.

"See that?" he asked Earl.

"What?" Earl said listlessly. He had been exceptionally quiet since the explosion. Carolina stopped the tape, rewound, and cued up the segment again.

"That," Carolina said. The camera, in the midst of a long, slow pan across the parade, had caught Molly Whipple in her scuffle with Chelsea's kidnapper. The image held up for only a few frames of video before Earl panned back to a group of Shriners.

"I saw this for a minute, just before he threw the dynamite."

"Know any of them?" Earl asked.

"That woman. She's supposed to be a local realtor."

The video showed the woman and her beefy companion after they had all collapsed in a heap.

"She bumped into the little guy with the beard."

"Pretty clumsy," Earl said.

"Wait," Carolina said. The image blurred slightly as Molly Whipple and the two men picked themselves up. "Does this thing have slo-mo?"

Earl reached over and flicked a switch on the underside of the control panel. A new playback deck and monitor lit up, next to the one Carolina was using.

"This was just installed a month ago. Kind of a makeshift job, but it works."

Carolina popped the tape from the player and slipped it into the new deck.

"It's going to take me a second to get this worked out," Earl said. At the same moment, there was a knock on the van's door. Carolina pressed the latch.

Ernie O'Mara peered inside, with Bert Schumacher directly behind him.

"Well, if it isn't my old friends," Carolina said.

Bert looked pained. Ernie simply stared.

"We heard you got tape," Bert said.

"You're welcome to see what's on the air," Carolina replied.

"We'd like to look at your raw video."

Carolina didn't answer. Earl kept working on the console, trying to rig the slo-mo deck. Ernie grew impatient.

"You know better than to fuck with a federal agent, Carolina."

"Going to shoot me again, O'Mara?"

Schumacher wiped his brow. "Ernie, go interview some witnesses."

"There aren't any more witnesses," Ernie protested.

"Then just go."

Ernie slipped away. Schumacher looked at Carolina. "Aren't you two ever going to be friends?"

"Not this month," Carolina said.

"I guess that's all right," Bert responded. "But I believe you've got a colleague missing."

"That's right."

"What was she doing up on that clam, anyway?"

"Spreading Channel Three's goodwill."

"Uh-huh," Bert said.

"It wasn't my idea," Carolina said.

"I'm sure. Listen, you probably know—"

"—that looking at the tape might help you find her. Yeah. Come on in."

Bert Schumacher climbed into the now-cramped van. While he did, Earl made the final hookup to get the new playback deck working.

"What are you looking at?" the ATF man asked.

Carolina explained as they rolled the tape again. The camera lens panned once across the crowd, and on to Molly Whipple and the two men. As the three of them started to rise, Carolina pressed a button and the flow of the tape slowed.

"What's that in her hand?" Earl said.

"Some kind of gun," Carolina said.

"Revolver," Bert answered. "Probably a .38. You know this woman?"

Forty-five minutes later a group of ATF agents and Providence and Cranston police officers executed a no-knock warrant on the Whipple Realty agency on Elmwood Avenue. No one was inside, so the offices were quickly secured and a search commenced. Carolina and Earl were kept outside for the first ten minutes, before Schumacher came out.

"What have you got?" Carolina asked.

"We got shit," Bert said. "No guns, no bombs. No friggin' dynamite. The search is a wash."

There was something about his tone that held Carolina's attention.

"Is there anything you're not telling me?"

"Yeah."

"Such as?"

The agent smirked. "This Thelma Pitts you been telling me about. The one with a boat registered to this address?"

Carolina nodded.

"She's got a record."

"Federal?"

"Yeah. West Coast. She used to work the casinos in Reno. Blackjack dealer, back in the late seventies."

Carolina leaned forward.

"You know what capping is?" Schumacher asked.

Carolina paused for a second. "I've heard of it."

"Well, that's what she was into. Got thrown out of Reno. Couldn't work Vegas, either, 'cause the casinos were too close."

"So what happened?"

"Word has it she got tied in with the Gambino family in New York. FBI in Brooklyn had her as a suspect in a hit there four, five years back. But they never had enough evidence. Then she disappeared."

"Until she showed up here."

Schumacher nodded.

"Do you have a picture of this lady?"

A dark blue sedan pulled over to the curb as Carolina asked the question. Bert Schumacher looked over as Ernie O'Mara climbed out, a manila folder in his hand.

"I sent him back to the office to get one faxed over."

Ernie walked up and handed Schumacher the folder, offering Carolina a tough look. Carolina smiled sweetly. Ernie shook his head and walked into the real estate office.

"Was he beaten as a child?" Carolina asked.

"Naw," Bert said. "He's just sore he never made the cut for the FBI."

"How tragic."

"To him it is," Schumacher said. He withdrew a piece of fax paper from the folder. As Carolina reached to take it Earl came walking up.

"Shirley's on the phone. Says you've got to be back at the blast site by six."

"I'll be there," Carolina said.

"If you don't you're fired."

"She always says that," Carolina said.

"Yeah, but she sounds serious."

Carolina examined the paper. The grainy photograph was old, blurred by the facsimile transmission.

"You know her?" Schumacher asked.

"You could say that," Carolina said. "Say hello to Ms. Molly Whipple."

William Markey was heading into Pawtuxet Cove after a hot afternoon on the bay. He had been raking clean beds just north of Prudence Island since just after sunrise, and his boat was full. The heat had driven all but the hardiest quahoggers off the water, and William was happy to have so much territory to himself.

So happy that he almost missed the dirty gray skiff blasting south, kicking spray and leaving a broad green wake behind her. Like many clam boats, the skiff was overpowered, with huge outboard engines designed for a boat of much larger size.

Markey knew the boat. He recognized the sloppy paint job and the strange way the tiny cabin house slanted to one side. As the boat roared past, he even recognized the registration letters on the little ship's bow.

What William Markey did not recognize was the man driving the skiff. He was short, with wild hair and a wild beard, and gave no sign of acknowledgment as he blew down the channel from Providence like a flat skipping stone.

This was troubling to Markey, because he knew that the owner of the skiff, Rick Deasle, was not working. He'd broken a leg a week earlier, and Markey knew Deasle wasn't the type to lend his skiff while his leg was on the mend.

Markey picked up the VHF radio he kept onboard and called on Channel 16. Deasle answered within seconds.

"How's the leg, Ricky?"

"Hot and itchy with this weather. Be glad to get this friggin' cast off. Hey, y'missed a helluva show at the parade today. Some guy set off a load of dynamite, blew up half of Cranston."

"Izzat right?" Markey exclaimed. "Well, I just been watchin' a show of my own."

"Really?"

"Think so. You lend anyone your boat today?"

"Course not."

"Didn't think so. Listen, you better call the cops then. I think somebody just stole it."

Deasle, cursing, switched off almost immediately. Markey thought of turning around and giving chase. But he knew his engine couldn't match the high-powered ones on Deasle's boat, especially not with a full load of clams on board. What settled the matter was the nasty purple speedboat that blew by him a few seconds later, narrowly missing his boat and sending off a wake that nearly swamped his skiff. Markey yelled, but the skinny woman and huge man at the helm of the race boat paid him no attention. Markey struggled to keep his clam buckets from falling overboard, and pondered the risks associated with being a good Samaritan.

19

All three Providence stations led the Saturday evening broadcast with details from the *Gaspee* Parade explosion. The anchors spoke in low tones, each looking pained as they described the mayhem wrought by the man everyone now called the Quahog Bomber. The anchors on Channels Nine and Thirteen both referred to Chelsea Alvarez as a "local television personality" without naming her station. Channel Three more than made up for the omission of the other stations, running a graphic bearing the legend "The Hunt for Our Little Chelsea," and an interview with the general manager, who tearfully explained what an asset Chelsea was to the station, and how much she loved Providence. Grudgingly, the GM also announced that Channel Three would offer a five-thousand-dollar reward to anyone with information that would lead to Chelsea's safe recovery.

Carolina's piece eclipsed the coverage on the competing stations, with powerful images of the explosion and video of the ATF search of Whipple Realty. As Earl's tape rolled past Mitty Navel and Thelma Pitts, Carolina explained that the authorities were now investigating the connection between the would-be realtor and the clamdigger.

The weekend anchor, a handsome young man from Fall River who vowed openly that he would be working at ABC before he was thirty, tried to appear unimpressed.

"Good piece, Mike. How did you feel when the bomb went off?"

Carolina stared blankly at the camera for a moment.

"Like I wanted to wet my pants," he said, finally.

"Uh, thanks, Mike." The anchor moved on to another story.

"You're clear," Earl said, grinning.

"Kid'll go far with that kind of question."

Earl nodded. "He's ready for network right now."

The microwave van's cell phone rang.

"Bet that's Shirley calling to chew you out," Earl said.

"Sorry," Carolina said when he picked up. "The kid gave me an opening and I had to take it."

"Well, I hope she was over sixteen," Carla said.

Carolina paused. "I thought you were someone else."

"I bet you did."

"Really."

"I believe you. Been listening to the radio. You've been at the parade?"

"Oh, yeah," Carolina said.

"Get any good pictures?"

"You could say that," he said, smiling. "Where are you?"

"Down near Wickford. It's been a slow day." Indeed it had. Carla had written just one citation that day, to a powerboater caught dumping the contents of a marine toilet over the side of his boat. The man had cursed her heartily. Carla just smiled and wished him a pleasant afternoon as she handed him the ticket.

"When does your shift end?"

"I've got to stay on this story tonight, at least 'til eleven. What did you have in mind?"

"I thought I might go hang around Thayer Street," Carla said. "Maybe see if I could pick up a reporter."

"Really?" Carolina said. "I thought cops hated reporters."

"I'm trying to broaden my horizons."

"I see. You know, I like Thayer Street."

"Do you now?"

"Yeah. There's a little Indian restaurant. Place called Kabob 'N Curry. Serves terrific barra-kabob."

"What's barra kabob?" Carla asked.

"You've never had barra-kabob? You should try it."

"What then?"

"That depends. If they haven't caught the quahog bomber, I thought I might pick up a cop, maybe bring her home to watch videos."

"In place of looking at your etchings?"

"Exactly."

Carla laughed gently. Carolina liked the sound. "I get off in an hour," she said. "But a dispatcher just called about a report of a stolen clam boat. I need to take a spin around the islands."

"That's fine," Carolina said. It would leave him with enough time to put together a piece for the eleven o'clock broadcast.

"Call you in an hour at the station?"

"I'll be waiting," Carolina said.

Salt.

Chelsea Alvarez smelled it in the air, tasted it when she licked her lips. It was mild at first, then stronger, so pungent and biting that she could not stand it, and opened her eyes. All she saw were shells and dirt. And water. Salt water, lapping the shoreline.

She moved her head, and felt the piece of driftwood underneath it, a hard pillow on the rocky beach. Oddly, it was comfortable, as long as she didn't move too much.

"Where—?"

A noise in front of her made her jump. The sound of shoes scuffing against shells. She pulled herself up and stared, too frightened and tired to scream.

Mitty Navel stared back. He held a plastic bucket in one hand, and cradled a small load of driftwood with his other arm. He let the driftwood drop, and the pieces fell haphazardly, clattering against the rocky ground and one another. Mitty ignored the sound. He did not take his eyes off the young weather girl.

Chelsea looked down, saw that her hands and feet were free, but that her clothes were covered with feathers and markings that looked like white chalk. She looked up again into the eyes of the wild-haired man. They were black and piercing. He looked powerful. But the expression on his face was gentle.

"Where are we?" she asked.

"Sank-sherry."

"Where?" She stood up. The sun was fading rapidly, kicking up a magnificent orange glare on the bay. There were no houses, no cars or signs of other people.

"Island," Mitty said. He waved an arm around. "Sank-sherry. Berrrds." He fell to his knees, and began to dig with his bare hands. Chelsea looked around, and as the sun weakened, the glare eased enough to make her understand.

Birds. They were everywhere. Loons. A few herons. But mostly seagulls, hundreds of seagulls, all of them nestled or squatting, staring at them with fierce expressions as Mitty continued to dig.

"What are chew doing?" she asked.

"Dug clams," he grunted. "I'll make a pit and steam 'em." He pointed at the driftwood pile beside him. "Then we can eat."

Chelsea almost gagged at the thought. Unconsciously she began to swat the feathers from her clothes, watching Navel and wondering how she could get away. When most of the feathers had fallen away she started to work on the chalk stains. They had dried, hard and fast, and were difficult to remove. In the twilight she stopped for a moment to look at a seagull. A moment before the bird had looked angry. Now it almost seemed to grin.

It was then that Chelsea realized what the chalk stains were.

"I chust hate Rhode Island," she whined.

Carla Tattaglia's police boat planed easily across the open water. The sea had been almost flat throughout the hot day, but with twilight the temperature dropped, the breeze picked up, and the speed of the boat made it seem cooler than it was. Carla removed her hat and loosened her hair until it fell softly across her shoulders, then fluttered behind her. A little wind was therapeutic.

She made a pass around Patience, slipping through the slender cut that separated the island from her larger sister, Prudence. She did a slow cruise around the bigger island, stopping briefly in Potter's Cove. A few sail and powerboats were anchored for the evening, but there was no sign of a clam skiff. Carla turned south, down the bay's east passage, watching the lights begin to wink on-shore.

The sky overhead was the color of ripe peaches, blending into a swirl of red and then deep blue just before the horizon. Carla kept the engine at low throttle, listening to the water and the soft hum of the motor. The calm that had descended on Narragansett Bay made the unpleasant aspects of her job worthwhile.

At the southern tip of Prudence she turned west, back toward Wickford, before heading north toward Greenwich Bay. It was a beautiful evening, but there was no one else on the water. The search for the missing clam boat was clearly a wash.

Just off Wickford Harbor is a tiny island, uninhabited by all but a few birds and a seal or two. The island is called Hope, and it offers local wild life refuge from the marine traffic that plies the western part of Narragansett Bay.

Which did nothing to explain the smoke, of course.

Carla noticed the wisps snaking into the now pink and purple sky. It was not the first time. Too often, she'd had to chase off would-be campers, usually teenagers who planned to spend the evening drinking or smoking and occasionally fornicating.

She swung the boat toward the island for a closer look. The source of the smoke was hidden from view, on the island's western side. It wasn't until she was just a few hundred yards off that she noticed the clam skiff, pulled up on the beach of the island's eastern shore.

That and the big purple cigarette boat bobbing at anchor.

20

Paulie Colasanto was definitely in love.

He loved the way that Thelma Pitts took charge, made decisions, told him what to do. Loved the way she handled a gun. Loved the way she held herself when she was following the little dork carrying the screaming Latina chick and the dynamite. He even loved the way she clutched herself whenever she felt cold. Which she apparently did right now, the way she was clawing at her shoulders in the gathering darkness.

And maybe, just maybe, she loved him, too. Ever since that moment on the boat out on the sound, the night Libby caught one behind the ear. It could've been me, he thought. But she didn't. She kept me around.

Thelma Pitts said nothing to him as they followed Navel through the screaming crowd, running from the dynamite stick and the smoke and the raining pieces of clam-colored papier-mâché. But then, she didn't have to. He followed like a lapdog, hanging on her every word, watching each move that she made.

He'd wondered what it might be like to be with her. To spend a little time in a casino, or off in one of those love nests in the Poconos, the ones with the heart-shaped tubs and mirrors on the ceiling. She'd like a place like that, he knew it. If only they could find the right time. The right spot.

After all, she said she wanted Mr. Goodbar, he thought.

"Shit."

Thelma's curse brought him back to reality. She didn't like

climbing around on this scuzzy little island, all covered with rocks and—crap.

"Look what I got on my shoe," she muttered.

A few feet away a seagull opened its beak and screamed at the two of them for invading its turf. The bird picked itself up and pushed off, flapping twice, then gliding a few feet more before settling down again. The bird threw them a baleful glare.

"Youse want I should shoot it?" Paulie asked.

Thelma marveled at the man's stupidity and shook her head.

Mitty Navel built his fire at the bottom of the hollowed-out pit. When the driftwood was reduced to coals, he took a rag from the bucket, soaked it in the sea, wrung it out, and laid the rag gently over the pit. Immediately the coals began to hiss and steam shot into the air. Mitty poured the bucket of clams on top and began covering the pit with rocks. Chelsea watched in horrified fascination.

"What's that?"

Mitty smiled proudly and grinned as steam and smoke rose past his face.

"Fuggin' clams," he said. "Shore dinner."

"I theenk I'm gonna be seek."

"Good with beer," Mitty said. "Cold beer."

"I want to go home."

"Can't. Sank-sherry." Mitty's mind had not quite sorted through the events of the day. The parade, the teeming crowd, and the heat were all a blur. Still, the memory of a woman with a gun penetrated the dense fog in his mind. The gun, and the gargantuan quahog that he had defeated in battle. All with the aid of the dynamite sticks.

The sticks. That he'd left in the boat.

Mitty felt the danger before he saw it. But without the dynamite, he was naked.

"Looking for something, scumbag?" Thelma Pitts asked sweetly.

* * *

The package was vivid, starting with the parade and moving almost immediately to the powerful video from the explosion.

"You'll get an Emmy for this, my friend," Carolina said.

Earl nodded modestly. "You weren't so bad yourself. Nobody else got that search warrant stuff."

Carolina shifted on his seat inside the cramped editing booth. It was past nine, and there were few others in the station. "I wonder where Chelsea is?"

"You've asked that three times. If I were you, I'd wait before calling the cops again."

Carolina nodded. He watched as the taped package came to a close. One minute fifty-three seconds. An eternity for a local broadcast.

"Can I ask you something?" Earl said.

"Fire away."

"Do you still get the rush?"

"The rush?"

Earl pointed at the screen. "You know. From this. The work."

Carolina looked down at the printed script in his hand, then back at the tape. It was rewinding now, at high speed, the words and pictures a blurry electronic mess, with voices and images thrown into chaos until the tape slowed and stopped, frozen on the image of Channel Three's logo superimposed over color bars and a countdown.

"When you start out," he said slowly, "everything is a rush. The fires, the shootings, even the press conferences with the politicians."

"I remember," Earl said. "That was thirty years ago for me."

"But after a while, it starts to blend together. Every story seems to be the same. The embattled politician always offers a lame excuse or says no comment. The cops never loosen up. The widows always cry."

He pressed the EJECT button on the machine, and waited for the recorder to spit out the cassette.

"But then, just when you think you've seen every story before, that no original comments or ideas are left, a quahog bomber walks into frame."

Earl started laughing. Carolina smiled. "And he just destroys that neat little theory."

Carolina scribbled on a label, peeled the back off, and laid it on the cassette. "I still get the rush," he said. "It doesn't come as often. It doesn't always last as long. But I still get it."

"So nice to hear you saying that," Shirley said.

Carolina turned. "You're here late."

"I've got an employee missing, and a huge story breaking."

"Nice to know you care," Carolina said.

"You both did a fantastic job today," Shirley said.

"Thanks," Earl said. He took the cassette from Carolina's hand. "I'll bring this over to ENG." Earl winked and slipped out the door.

"We could have done without the 'wet my pants' line, Michael."

"I know," Carolina said. "But it was such a stupid question."

"Yes it was. But you know how this game is played. We all have to support each other."

"Sorry."

"Uh-huh." She looked at him.

"It won't happen again."

"Yes it will."

He looked at her.

"You're probably right."

Shirley sighed. "You're one of the best reporters I've ever met. But you don't take supervision well."

"I thought this was Rhode Island," Carolina said. "You know, home of the independent man?"

"Don't get smart with me," she said. "We still need to work as a team." She sat down in the seat next to him. She looked tired.

"You may not believe this, but I have spent considerable time trying to save your ass."

Carolina raised an eyebrow. "The general manager again?"

Shirley nodded. "Every time you make some smug remark. Every time you take off to check out some lead and we wind up a package short at six o'clock. Every time, I hear about it."

"You want me to talk to him?"

"God no, the two of you would probably wind up killing each other." Shirley sighed, then rubbed her hand across her chin.

"I wanted to be a journalist," she said.

"You are."

She smiled. "Bullshit. I'm a manager. A news manager. I worry about ratings and budgets and keeping people happy. Yes, I make some decisions about stories and how to cover them. But I'm not out tracking down the material. Watching it happen and telling people about it."

It was quiet in the editing booth, the two of them thinking for a moment.

"My point," Shirley said finally, "is that you're a lot luckier than you realize. You do your job well. But all the window dressing, all the crap—that's the price you pay for that rush you were telling Earl about."

"Does this mean I have to do the weather tonight?" Carolina smiled. Shirley tried to keep a straight face, but couldn't.

"I'll think about what you said, Shirl."

Shirley gazed at the tape cassette in Carolina's hand. "Have you followed up on Chelsea?"

Carolina nodded. "I called ATF, Cranston police. Earl's been listening to the scanners. We grabbed video of the police going door to door in Cranston before we came back here. Have you talked to anyone?"

"I just got off the phone with Chelsea's father," Shirley said. "He started crying. Then he threatened to sue us for sending his daughter on such a dangerous assignment."

"Wonderful." Carolina looked at the wall clock. Nine fifteen.

"I'm going to call ATF again," he said.

Carolina let the phone ring twenty times. He called Cranston police again. A sullen dispatcher put him through to detectives.

"Franco," a voice said. The tension pulsed through the telephone like a wave.

"Captain, Michael Carolina from Channel Three."

"Can't talk, Mike," Franco said, and hung up.

Carolina walked over to the assignment desk. A gaunt-looking assignment editor, just six months out of journalism school and brand-new to the station, was listening to the scanners. Earl stood behind him.

"What are you hearing?" Carolina asked.

"Got some traffic on the low-level frequencies," the young editor said.

"The ones the cops think we can't receive," Earl said. "Something's going down on the water, near Hope Island."

21

itty was on his knees.

"Hit him again," Thelma commanded.

Paulie reached down and hauled Navel up by the front of his shirt. He laid another punch into the little man's rib cage, knocking him down once more. Paulie turned and gazed lustily at Thelma. She ignored the look.

"So what was it?" she asked. "Who sent you?"

Mitty did not respond. He stared at the two of them, his eyes dry and empty. He let out a small groan.

"Come on," Thelma said. "All I want to know is what you were doing there."

Mitty said nothing. Thelma leaned over him, then backed away.

"God, he stinks."

"I don't smell nothin'," Paulie said.

Chelsea Alvarez, huddled next to a large rock, rolled her eyes. She could smell Mitty Navel from ten feet away. The three of them—the woman, the big man, and the tiny clamdigger were silhouettes, backlit by the last rays of twilight. Chelsea felt nauseous.

"Whyn't youse shoot his knee?" Paulie offered helpfully.

Thelma had already given the idea some thought, and dismissed it as lacking creativity. She also feared the muzzle flash. The gun was tucked inside her waistband.

She looked around for a moment and noticed Chelsea lying on the ground. Briefly, she considered ordering Paulie to break a finger or two. But the woman looked half-dead to begin with. And given that the little man had kidnapped her, it was hard to believe he'd care if Paulie worked her over.

Then she felt the steam.

It wafted up from a pile of rocks, scented of kelp and clams. A completely unique odor. Thelma reached down and found a stick, then pushed the rocks away. Finally, she found what she was looking for.

"Havin' a little clambake, uh?"

Mitty said nothing.

"Paulie," Thelma said, "ever see a guy with a hot clam in his pants?"

Paulie wasn't sure what she meant. He looked down, embarrassed, at his own shorts, then gave a small sigh of relief. "No," he said.

"Neither have I," Thelma said. "But I think we should find out."

She found another stick, then rummaged through the clam pile as Paulie took hold of Navel. The quahogger's eyes grew wide, and he squirmed, but still said nothing. Thelma held the two pieces of driftwood like giant chopsticks, lifting a fat quahog out of the pile.

"Chew are sick," Chelsea said, horrified. She gave out a little cry.

"Shut up," Thelma said, "or I'll try it out on you."

She walked toward Mitty, holding the sticks in one hand, the steaming clam between them. "Okay, scumbag," she said, "one more time. Tell us what you were doing in the cove, or cherrystones are gonna take on a whole new meaning."

Mitty was in shock. The woman looked hideous, the sticks and the hot clam like some giant claw reaching out to maim him.

"Fuggin' clams," he muttered.

Thelma moved closer. "What?"

" 'Z'fuggin' clams. My bed. My bed."

She stopped for a minute, the sticks and the quahog poised in midair. "Huh?"

"He was in my bed," Mitty mumbled. "Messin' with my turf."

"Your turf?" Thelma said. "That's bullshit. Who sent you?"

"Was my bed," Mitty repeated.

Thelma reached with her free hand for the waist of Mitty's pants.

"Who sent you?"

The launch tore across the water. Earl struggled to keep his camera secure while Carolina held on to the boat's center console.

"You sure your station's good for this?" the driver said. He was a man in his mid-forties, who'd been cleaning out his boat at the Wickford dock.

"I gave you a credit card number," Carolina said.

"I know," the man said. "But you guys are number three in the ratings."

"That's why we try harder," Earl said. "Just drive." The photographer put his hand on Carolina's shoulder. "You all right?"

Carolina looked at him. "What do you mean?"

"You didn't say a word on the way down here."

"There's a lot to think about," Carolina said.

The truth, Carolina knew, was that he was wondering where Carla was. The calls on the scanner did not say if she was on the island. There was no way to know if she was armed. Or whether anyone else on the island might be.

"I just hope you guys got this covered," the driver muttered again.

Earl leaned over toward the driver. "We told you, chief, it's covered. If it isn't, you can have my friggin' camera. Now shut up and drive this sucker."

"You don't have to yell," the driver said.

Two thousand yards to the northeast, two more launches planed across the water. One was filled with officers from Cranston and Rhode Island State Police, including a pair of police divers. The other was loaded with four ATF agents. The ATF boat spanked the water, bumping and tossing three of the federal officers, who threw baleful looks at the fourth. He drove wildly, jerking the launch's wheel, wind in his hair, oblivious to the mild suffering of his companions.

"You sure you've done this before?" Bert Schumacher said.

Ernie ignored him. He was having too much fun. They were charging into battle, and he was leading.

"Hope Island is southwest," Bert shouted over the noise of the engine and the rush of the wind.

"I know that," Ernie said.

"Doesn't look that way," Bert said. "You got the boat pointed toward Newport."

Ernie instantly threw the wheel to the right, nearly knocking one of the agents out of the boat.

"Christ, O'Mara," he growled, "if you pull another jackass stunt like that I'll drown you myself."

"It's the currents," Ernie said. "They're wild out here."

"That's bullshit," the other federal officer said. "Why don't you let one of us drive?"

Ernie again ignored the remark. "Why don't you men check your loads? We may need some firepower in a while."

The ATF agent who'd nearly been thrown from the boat leaned over toward Bert and nodded toward Ernie. "How the hell did he ever make the Bureau?" he whispered.

Carla didn't want to confront the strange gathering on the Hope Island beach. At least, not without some backup.

She'd called in the moment she sighted the two boats anchored off the island. Dispatch told her to hold on, that support was on the way. But Carla waited twenty minutes, then a half hour, and there was no sign of help.

She felt uneasy not knowing what was taking place on the other side of the island, afraid to circle it in her boat, for fear it would alert whoever was on shore. Carla was almost certain that Mitty Navel was nearby. The description of the man driving the stolen clam boat was too close. Based on the description of the parade's events, Carla was equally convinced that Mitty had access to a substantial amount of dynamite. The situation was not to be taken lightly.

After thirty minutes, Carla called in on her radio again, asking for the location of her backup. They're on their way, sit tight, she was told. Still in her own DEM boat, Carla shifted from idle to low throttle, and eased her way over to the clam boat, training the spotlight on the interior. The little boat was empty. She played the spot over the registration numbers painted on the bow, then checked them against the report she'd received. It was definitely the stolen boat.

The clues were too much. Carla pointed her boat toward shore, cut the engine, and glided in until the water was hip deep. She threw out a small anchor, grabbed a Mossberg twelve-gauge shotgun, and eased over the side. She was ashore in a minute. A few gulls, settling in for the evening, gave her a quick look, then turned away. She listened for voices. And heard them.

In a moment she was moving up toward the little island's higher ground. She stopped to listen again, and was drawn toward the sound of the voices. The rocks made it hard to walk, but Carla managed to keep quiet. In a moment she came over a crest, and there, perhaps forty feet away, were three silhouettes: a big, beefy man holding a smaller one, and a woman with sticks in her hand.

"Who sent you?" the woman demanded. She held the sticks closer to the little man. "Who?"

Carla announced her presence not with her voice but with a sound.

The noise made when the trigger is cocked on a .38 revolver is unique. It is a sound with two distinct clicks, indicating that the weapon is ready to fire. To those who are familiar with it, the noise can be disconcerting, if not downright terrifying.

171

Thelma Pitts was indeed familiar with the noise. So was Paulie. Thelma flinched, then turned her head to the left. Paulie relaxed, ever so slightly.

Mitty Navel was not familiar with the sound of a .38. He did not relax. He concentrated on the still steaming clam held between the two sticks, the one Thelma proposed to drop inside his pants. As Thelma turned and Paulie eased his grip Mitty kicked with everything he had. The sticks went flying. Paulie cursed.

And Thelma Pitts let out a long, low shriek as the hot quahog seared the left side of her face.

The new sound made Paulie relax even more, and Mitty Navel brought one of his kicking legs back down, hard, onto Paulie's instep. He howled, and Mitty struggled free.

In the midst of it all Carla Tattaglia trained a flashlight on them and shouted, "Police! Freeze!"

No one listened. Paulie jumped up and down on his one good foot. Thelma Pitts writhed in pain, holding her hands to her face. And Mitty ran for Chelsea. He picked her up and started to run, paying no attention as she slapped him feebly on the back and arms.

Carla set the flashlight down and moved to the right. She held the revolver steady, keeping it trained on the three people in front of her.

"Lie down," she commanded. "All of you."

Mitty kept moving, and Carla knew there was nothing she could do. Paulie, the pain easing enough to comprehend, dropped awkwardly to his knees.

Thelma Pitts continued to hold her face.

"It hurts, oh, it hurts."

"Lie down. Do it now."

Thelma moved her hand away, to reveal a small mass of charred, swelling flesh. She looked around for the source of the voice ordering her to the ground.

"My God, it hurts."

Carla watched her. "I'm not going to tell you again."

"But it hurts," Thelma said, reaching for her waistband.

The moment Carla saw the gun she put a round into Thelma Pitts's right elbow. The force shattered the bone, and sent Thelma's weapon bouncing on the rocks and shells.

Finally, Thelma decided to lie down.

Carla kept her revolver trained on the injured woman. Thelma no longer exaggerated cries of pain, instead offering the real thing as she stared at her mangled arm. Carla moved forward, her eyes never leaving Pitts, until she was close enough to kick Pitts's own weapon farther across the rocks.

Carla felt the bullet strike just above her right hip. The force spun her to the right, just enough to avoid the second one. She turned, almost by instinct, and emptied three more rounds into Paulie's head. Paulie died with his own pistol still clutched between his two meaty hands.

Carla looked back at Thelma, who had fallen silent. She moved her .38 into her left hand, then touched her side until it felt slippery. Slowly, Carla slid to the ground, still training her gun on Thelma Pitts as a speedboat searchlight played across Hope Island's rocky shore.

"This is so hard," Carla whispered to herself. The light was hot, white, and intense. When it found Paulie, it made his face seem like a bad jigsaw puzzle divided into broken pieces of black and white. Thelma started to moan again.

Carla sighed once more. "Really," she said to no one, "this is so hard."

Mitty bounded over the rocks, ignoring the gunshots. Chelsea still flailed at his back.

"Stop," she gasped. "Chu have to stop."

Mitty didn't listen. He half stumbled from the weight of the tiny weather girl bearing down on his shoulders. The boat. He had to get to the boat.

There were more shots, and the peace of the still waters was interrupted by the sound of engines. Boat engines. Mitty reached the beach. Chelsea was still trying to talk him into putting her down. Instead he waded waist-high into the water until he reached the side of the clam boat. Mitty dumped Chelsea unceremoniously into the skiff and yanked hard at the anchor line running to the shore. It came loose after three tugs, and Mitty heaved himself aboard.

"Where are we going?" Chelsea cried. Mitty didn't stop to look at her. Instead he checked the battery and pressed the ignition key. The little skiff's oversized engines grunted, spat, and then roared as he laid into the throttle. But the boat didn't move. It was not yet in gear.

More engine noises emerged from the darkness, followed by more spotlights. A voice shouted. Mitty reached for the bag he'd been carrying before, and drew out another stick of dynamite.

"Sank-sherry," he said. "Sank-sherry."

He dug in a pocket for a light and would have found it had Chelsea not found the oar. The owner kept it loose along the skiff's gunwale, for those unpleasant moments when the engine died. Chelsea caught him full in the face with it.

The force knocked Mitty Navel off his feet, and the dynamite stick rolled, unlit, across the sole of the skiff. Chelsea did not stop to watch what happened. Still screaming, she jumped into the water and started swimming toward shore.

"There he is!" Ernie cried, overwhelmed by the excitement.

"Then slow the fuckin' boat down," Bert growled, reaching for a bullhorn. O'Mara saw it and grabbed it.

The launch carrying the ATF agents was slowing rapidly, casting a broad wake off both sides of the bow. The water rolled in toward the little clam skiff as Ernie raised the bullhorn to his lips.

"This is the ATF. I repeat, this is the ATF. Heave to. Heave to and raise your hands." Ernie paused for a second, unsure if he'd said all the right things. "Uh, heave to, raise your hands, cut your engine, and prepare to be boarded. How's that?" He turned and looked at Bert.

"Give me that thing," Bert said, snatching the bullhorn away from Ernie.

"Shit, he's running," one of the other agents said. Indeed, the clam skiff let out a roar and turned directly into the path of the ATF launch.

In an instant Ernie O'Mara drew his nine-millimeter. He fired three shots in the direction of the clam skiff. The two agents in the back of the boat yelled for him to stop. Bert ignored them. He reached for the console and threw the engine back into gear. The clam skiff was bearing down, just a few yards away and picking up speed. Ernie fired another round.

Bert shoved the throttle forward and pulled the wheel to the right. The launch rocked, bobbed, then twisted. It missed the accelerating clam skiff by inches. Ernie, off balance, fell over the side.

"Help!" he called, still hanging on to a cleat off the launch's port side. The two agents from the stern ignored him. Bert cursed again, then disengaged the engine once more. With one hand he hauled his partner back aboard.

"Thanks, Bert," the young agent said. Bert ignored the words, and instead grabbed for the weapon still clutched in Ernie's right hand.

"What are you doing?" Ernie asked. Bert released the clip from the nine-millimeter and tossed it over the side. He practically threw the pistol back to his partner, then returned to the console.

"You threw my load in the water," Ernie said, crestfallen.

Bert Schumacher threw the engine back in gear.

"If you say another word, I'll do the same thing to you."

The ATF launch shot forward once again, in pursuit of the clam boat, now one hundred yards ahead of them. The Cranston police boat, which had observed the strange behavior of the skiff and the ATF agents, was right behind them. Bert pushed the throttle as far as it could go. One of the other ATF agents stepped forward and shouted above the engine roar.

"Think Wyatt Earp here hit that guy?"

"How the fuck do I know?" Bert answered.

The clam skiff was now in high gear, the police boat and the agents closing in behind.

Mitty Navel was in agony, his collarbone shaved by one of the bullets from Ernie O'Mara's pistol. He drove blind, heading due north. Back toward Pawtuxet and Stillhouse Cove.

All he wanted was a place to go, a place to hide.

"Sank-sherry," he mumbled. "Sank-sherry."

He never saw the shoals. They were marked on most charts, to be avoided at all times, but especially at low tide. In the near total darkness they rose like crusty talons from the bottom of the bay, waiting for someone unsuspecting to come along. They reached up and tore into the hull of the little skiff, sending it airborne. When the boat landed, the naked prop on the outboard kicked up a wide stream of sparks as it bounced along the rocks. The sparks in turn found the gasoline.

The burning gas quickly found what was left of the dynamite.

A man standing on a private beach on Prudence Island later described the sight. "It was like the birth of a star," he said, "all white and red and orange. It seemed so beautiful. Until you realized what it was."

A thousand yards to the south, Earl and Carolina were just stepping onto Hope Island. The light from the explosion lit the beach like the sun.

"My God," Earl said. For the second time that day, he trained his camera on a small-scale Armageddon. Carolina and the boat's driver stood, transfixed.

"Call for help, now!" For once, the boat's skipper did not argue with Carolina. He began to wade back toward the boat and its VHF.

The site grew more awesome, the flames still rippling into the sky, made larger still by the water's reflection. Earl kept rolling tape, using an oversized rock as an impromptu tripod. Carolina tried to imagine what it would be like at the center of the conflagration.

The noise was so faint they did not hear it at first. But as the rumbling from the explosion faded and the fire dimmed, Carolina turned his head. The sound was thin, reedy even, and might have been confused with the strange, rushing noises that wind makes on water. But there was no wind. The night remained almost dead calm.

Carolina looked at Earl, still intent on recording the images across the water. The boat's skipper waded back.

"I called for help," he said. "Coasties are on it."

"Do you hear anything?" Carolina asked.

The skipper gave him a strange look. "Just you," he said. "You wanna head over there and get some better film?"

"It's tape," Earl growled, "not film."

"Well, excuse me for trying to do you a favor," the skipper said. "I'll get my news from some other channel, thank you very much—" The man stopped when Carolina raised a hand to his lips, but still looked highly insulted. Carolina ignored him.

"I need your flashlight."

Grudgingly the skipper offered up the lamp he held in his left hand. "Some newsman you are. The story's out there."

But Carolina had already set off down the beach. He stopped twice, to listen again. Each time the noise was slightly louder, stronger, until it finally took on a recognizable sound.

Moans.

He saw the woman he knew as Molly Whipple first, her clothes bloody and her left hand still clutching at her face. Nearby lay the body of a large man, flat on his back, his upper torso a mess and his head all but gone.

He saw her last. She lay against a rock, her gun still in hand, eyes closed. Carolina knelt beside her, fighting hard to stop a wave of nausea and panic.

He touched her face with his hand. "Carla?"

She opened her eyes and managed a hint of a smile.

"Hey, Michael," she said softly.

He pulled her toward him, and she cried out. Then he saw the blood.

"We need some help over here!" he shouted, hoping Earl and the boat skipper were listening. He turned back to Carla.

"I'll get you out as soon as I can," he said. "You'll be fine." Then he wondered if what he'd said was true.

But Carla only smiled again. "I'm glad you made it," she said. "Am I going to be on the news?"

By sunrise the next morning every television station in Rhode Island, Hartford, and Boston had descended on Wickford. Each one chartered a boat and set out onto the bay to watch as a crew of Coast Guard cutters moved around a shoal-filled area half a mile north of Hope Island. A few stations, using the most advanced satellite and microwave technology, were able to obtain live pictures from the water. But as the sun rose and the temperatures again soared toward triple digits, there was very little to observe that would make interesting fodder for the evening broadcasts. The stolen clam boat that Mitty Navel rode to his death had disintegrated. The police boats used by the ATF and the Cranston police—what was left of them, anyway—had been hauled away by the Coast Guard in the middle of the night, before the local stations were able to scramble camera crews. Still the television crews remained on the water, in hopes that a body might be recovered, or that some strange piece of evidence might be fished from the sea.

Nothing was found, including any sign of Timothy Navel.

The real action for electronic journalists was no longer on the water, but at station assignment desks, where fierce competition was playing out.

"Nine and Thirteen both called three times this morning." The young assignment editor gulped a mouthful of lukewarm coffee. "They're absolutely *begging* for the tape."

Shirley smiled at the young man. His dark eyes carried rings the size of silver dollars, and nearly the same color.

"You ought to get some sleep," she said.

"I feel great," the young man said. "The network is still on hold. Two of the tabloids sent faxes, and another one's flooding my E-mail. I never knew how many people cared about a kidnapped weather girl."

"I'm just glad she's all right," Shirley said. A sopping wet Chelsea Alvarez had wandered over to the small crowd of boats and paramedics loading Carla Tattaglia and Thelma Pitts. She'd been admitted to the hospital for observation, and was by far the most minor casualty of the past evening.

"How are the cops?"

"Let's see," the young editor looked down at his notes. "There were two boats, according to the Coast Guard, one with Cranston cops and another loaded with ATF agents. The locals came out okay."

Shirley waited.

"The feds were more seriously hurt. Three out of the four were hospitalized. One's got a concussion. Another's in shock and has second-degree burns and a broken arm. The last one scarfed half a lungful of water, and suffered some broken ribs. They're all pretty lucky to be alive, I guess."

"That's good work," Shirley said. "Nice to see that Ocean State has taken us off the blacklist."

"Oh, I don't think so," the editor said. "This PR guy, Bleeder, he's not giving anything to us."

"Then how−?"

"Ever hear me do my impression of a Channel Nine reporter?" the editor asked. His tone was innocent, but his grin was malicious. "Stuart Bleeder said he was glad to help. Even made a point of telling me how much he was going to enjoy shutting down Channel Three on this one."

"I didn't hear that," Shirley said. "Don't ever let me hear that you've done something like that again." She leaned forward and patted him lightly on the shoulder. "Understand?"

The editor paused. "I think so."

"Good. Now where the hell is Carolina?"

"Haven't heard from him."

Shirley grimaced. "We have the only reporter within sight or sound of the biggest story of the summer, and now he takes a powder."

The nurse was busy, very busy. The caller had identified himself as a staff member in the CEO's office, and he said there would be a tour of the nursing stations in ten minutes. In a minor panic, she checked to make sure all the charts were in place, the medications stored. She never noticed the man slipping into the young policewoman's room at the end of the hall.

He moved toward the side of her bed, where she lay with her eyes still closed. Her face was pale and drawn, and a thin, clear tube ran into her nose. A thick bandage protruded from the side of a hospital gown.

Carolina looked at her. She was breathing softly, and a small wave of relief rushed over him. He wondered how it must have felt to take a bullet in the abdomen. How long it would take for her to recover.

"Is that you again?" He turned to look at the RN, staring angrily from the doorway. "I know who you are now, Mr. Bleeder warned us about you. The police are going to charge you with trespassing."

"You don't understand," Carolina said. "I'm not here for a story."

"I don't care why you're here. This is Intensive Care. And you just called with that phony story about a tour. I'm calling security right now."

"Please don't."

The nurse stopped. Carolina turned.

"I'd really like to talk to him," Carla whispered. "Please."

The nurse's tone changed as she spoke to her patient. "You've lost a lot of blood, and you need to rest. And I wouldn't trust this guy as far as I could throw him."

"I would," Carla said. The nurse stared at her. Then she turned to Carolina and tapped her watch.

"Two minutes. If you're not out of here then, I call security."

"If you hadn't found me—" Carla said when the nurse walked out.

"I'm just glad you're okay." He hadn't slept the entire night, wondering whether she would live. He had such a strong feeling for this woman with the dark hair and sparkling brown eyes. She had done things to his insides that he had never felt before. Not with Marie Brine. Not with Lilly. It was difficult to describe, but it was very special. He reached over and brushed her hand. Carla felt it, and turned her palm over until her hand was clasped gently in his.

"I remember some kind of explosion," she said.

"Your pal the clamdigger," he told her. "He nearly took out half the ATF agents in New England. Don't worry," he said, sensing her alarm. "I think they're going to make it."

"I don't know how to thank you," she said.

"You could start by letting me buy you dinner when you get out," he said. "And maybe we could work something else out, too."

Carla Tattaglia smiled. "Deal."

"I better get out of here before Nurse Ratchet calls the five-ohs." He bent down and kissed her lightly on the forehead. The nurse glared as he slipped out of the room.

"Wait right there," she said.

"Sorry," Carolina answered, "got a bus to catch." He could still hear the nurse yelling from two flights down on the emergency stairwell. But he did not leave the hospital. There was one more visit he had to pay.

Bert Schumacher was in another single room, sitting up and trying to eat a liquid breakfast. The eating went slow, because the act of swallowing made his ribs hurt. The sight of Carolina walking in did little to help his digestion.

"Hey, wonder boy. Hospital security know you're in here?"

"I'm glad it wasn't more serious," Carolina said, pointing to the bandages on the agent's ribs. "Want to tell me what happened?"

"We on the record?"

"Since you put it that way, I guess not."

"What happened is my partner, Ernie Captain Fuckin' Queeg O'Mara damn near got us all killed."

Schumacher explained how the Cranston police boat had turned because its driver had remembered the shoals. Ernie, at the helm of the ATF boat, had not.

"How bad were you hurt?"

"Ribs," the agent said, "I caught a little water, and some burns along the arm. I'll live long enough to kill my partner.

"Probably not," Schumacher sighed, "but it's nice to think about."

"Where is he?"

"Can you believe it? He's the only one came out of this without a scratch. The other two agents, they're a couple doors down the hall. I can't believe my fuckin' luck."

"Where's Thelma Pitts?"

"I hear they got her out of here in a hurry. She's locked up at the women's infirmary over at that new private detention center."

"So she wasn't hurt badly?"

"Fuck no, just a burn on her face and a shattered arm." Schumacher spoke casually, completely oblivious to the irony in his words.

Carolina checked his watch. Nine-fifteen. Security was probably combing the hospital looking for him by now. "Bert, I need a favor."

Schumacher snorted. "I'd laugh if it didn't hurt so much. What the hell should I do for you?"

"I'd like to know what you found inside that real estate office."

Schumacher stared at the ceiling for a moment, then adjusted himself once again in the hospital bed. The movement made him grimace.

"Truth is," he said, "I don't much like you. But you been fair with me. If I could give you something, I would. But there was so much paperwork, I didn't get to go through it."

"Paperwork?"

"Yeah, real estate stuff. They're bringing down some more agents from Boston today to inventory it, because with all the crap that happened last night, I didn't get a chance."

There was a noise at the door. Carolina turned to see two security officers. Stuart Bleeder stood behind them, hands on his hips.

"Mr. Carolina, we meet again."

"Pleasure's all yours, I'm sure."

Bleeder stepped into the room. "I want you to escort this man out of the building. If he tries to come in again, you hold him until I can summon the police."

The security guards took hold of Carolina's arms.

"He was just visiting me," Schumacher said. Bleeder turned and looked at him.

"You're the federal agent who can do whatever the fuck he wants, right?"

Schumacher smiled weakly and nodded.

"Wrong," Bleeder said. "Right now you're a patient. And this is my hospital, so I can do whatever the fuck *I* want. Since you're not related to this so-called journalist, he's out."

"Wonderful bedside manner," Carolina said.

"Get him out of here," Bleeder said.

"Hey, Mike," Bert Schumacher called.

"Yeah?" Carolina answered. But the guards wouldn't let him stop to talk. He was out the door and halfway down the hall when he heard Schumacher yell.

"Nine o'clock tomorrow morning. Rule 48-G! Hear me? 48-G!"

The guards didn't let go until Carolina was at the edge of Ocean State Hospital property. With the blast of heat and humidity, both of the security men were sweating heavily by the time they finished crossing the facility's parking lot to the place where Carolina had left his car.

"Thanks, guys," Carolina said. The guards did not leave. They offered surly looks and stood watching him.

Carolina started the engine and threw the Jeep into reverse. The guards, arms crossed, were waiting for him to drive off the hospital grounds. Carolina smiled.

"Merry Christmas." He roared off. In the rearview mirror he could see both of them wiping their foreheads with the sleeves of their blazers.

He was still worried about Carla. She had nearly died. But at least she was awake, and smiling. Those were good signs.

What was it that Bert Schumacher was trying to tell him? Rule 48-G. Nine in the morning. He repeated the phrases over and over to himself as the heat bore down on him and Sunday turned from morning to midday.

He returned to his apartment. The place was stifling, for he had turned the air-conditioning off before leaving Saturday morning. His answering machine signaled that he'd had multiple calls, but he didn't stop to listen, instead stripping off his clothes and heading straight for the shower. He turned the cold faucet all the way out, and let the water blast his back and chest while he thought again about what the ATF agent had said.

Rule 48-G. Nine in the morning.

Refreshed, he climbed out of the shower. The apartment's AC was kicking in, and he didn't perspire as he dressed again. He left the apartment before noon and drove straight back to the station. Rule 48-G.

"Where the hell have you been?" Shirley said, before he could get to his desk.

"Do we have a copy of the federal criminal code?" he asked.

"Why?"

"Just a hunch. Do we?"

The urgency of his question made Shirley forget for a moment that she was angry. She followed as Carolina walked over to the assignment desk. The young weekend editor, still dead on his feet and loving every minute of it, gave him a wicked smile.

"You got any idea how many people want to talk to you? I mean network called, tabloids, couple of Boston stations. Even that Jewish Puerto Rican guy from CNBC. They all want a package—"

"They all can wait," Carolina said, looking behind the young man's head. Carefully, he stepped behind the editor and plucked a volume off the shelf.

"I thought I'd seen one of these around," he said to himself.

Shirley and the editor watched him as he flipped through the pages. When he stopped, Shirley slipped behind him to look over his shoulder.

"Find something?" she asked.

"Tomorrow morning," he said.

Carolina cut two packages that afternoon: one for the network, another for the station's six o'clock broadcast. The pieces included all of Earl's video from the parade and then the footage of Mitty Navel vaporizing on Narragansett Bay. The pictures were spectacular, but there was very little explanation or context to explain them.

He called Carla in the evening. They spoke for only a few minutes, long enough for her to say she was indeed feeling better.

"When can you come visit me again?"

"When I know I won't be arrested," he responded.

He slept well, more from exhaustion than anything else. When his alarm went off he was instantly awake.

Carolina drove to Kennedy Plaza and parked by quarter to nine. He walked into the United States courthouse and through the metal detector.

"Ain't you that guy from Channel Three?" a white-haired court security officer asked him.

"Depends on why you're asking," Carolina said.

The officer laughed. "I seen you covering that clamcake bomber guy last night. Lemme tell ya, you're lucky to be walkin'."

"I appreciate your concern," Carolina said.

"Kid's got balls, I tell ya," the man said to his partner as Carolina hurried into the clerk's office.

The deputy clerk in charge of the desk was a man in his early fifties. "May I help you?"

"I'm looking for a return of service filed on a search warrant this morning. The warrant was executed over the weekend."

"Where?"

"Whipple Realty, Cranston."

The clerk disappeared for a moment. Carolina looked around the room, hoping that no other reporters would find their way into the office. He looked at the clock: 8:59 A.M.

The clerk returned and handed Carolina a thick sheaf of documents. He slipped into a cubbyhole to review them. Within three minutes he let out a whoop. The clerk looked up, startled.

"Anything wrong?" he asked.

"Not anymore," Carolina said.

He spent the next thirty minutes reviewing the documents and making copies. He was just wrapping up when he heard a familiar voice at the clerk's desk.

"Hello, Arthur," she said.

"Good morning, Ms. Brine. What can I do for you?"

"I need to see the return of service documents on a place called Whipple Realty."

"There's a lot of interest in that file," the clerk answered. "Someone's looking at it right now."

"That's all right," Carolina said. "I'm finished." He handed the papers to Brine. She looked tan, slender, and beautiful as ever, even as she struggled and then finally managed to erase any trace of astonishment from her face.

"You move quickly," she said.

"So do you. Who retained you, Jimmy Flannery or Thelma Pitts? Or was it both of them?"

Marie did not react. "I'm not sure I understand you," she said.

"I'm sure your client will," Carolina said. "Whoever it is, tell them that I'm going with a piece this evening about their plans to turn Stillhouse Cove into a waterfront casino."

Marie's brow was knit. "Excuse me?"

"Your client—or clients. ATF seized a ton of documents from Whipple Realty this weekend. That's the inventory. I've been trying to figure out why Whipple Realty had such a lock on the properties being sold around Stillhouse Cove ever since the day that diver got blown up. You remember that day, don't you?"

Marie Brine gave him a dark look. Carolina smiled innocently.

"They're going to call it Gaspee Gallery, after the ship. You know the story I'm talking about? Well, it doesn't matter." Carolina looked down at some of the documents he'd copied. "They had some preliminary site drawings, a draft prospectus for investors, even some stationery. And they've been quietly buying up every house on the market near the cove while they wait for the gambling referendum to go through in the fall."

"I really don't know what you're talking about," Marie said.

"I'm talking about your clients getting ready to cash in, Marie. I'm talking about that diver who got his eardrums blasted out, and then died while he was lying in a hospital bed. His name was Tony Palumbo, and he was a former dealer down at Bearclaw who got fired for capping cards. He was also into scuba, and he went to work for Molly Whipple, according to some of the letters seized in the inventory. Underwater surveying, testing the bottom of the cove to see how it would stand up to underwater construction. If you build a waterfront casino, you're going to need some pilings for dock space, maybe even a pier or a boardwalk to accommodate some of the boats carrying the high rollers. It would look great to the gamblers, but it would play hell on the clam beds."

The clerk was watching them, obviously finding the dialogue

more interesting than any work that needed to be done. Marie continued to hold the documents in her hand. She waited.

"I guess no one counted on a guy like Mitty Navel caring so much about that cove, or at least about his clams. I'm sure no one expected him to care enough to try and blast Tony Palumbo out of the water."

Marie was an exceptional attorney, Carolina knew, but they had a past. It was over perhaps, but in the time they'd been together he'd learned a little about how to set her off.

"That's why Thelma—or Molly, depending on when you met her—and her goon wanted to talk to him. To find out why he was tossing dynamite at their diver. And probably to make sure he wouldn't be able to do it again."

"You're just speculating, Michael. You don't know—" She caught herself. But some damage had been done.

"How would you know that, Marie? Someone been talking to you about this mess?"

Marie Brine said nothing more.

"Nobody realized how hard it would be to catch that little clamdigger. That he'd put up such a fight. It's too bad all these people had to buy it just so Jimmy Flannery and his partner could get rid of some complications."

Marie looked at him again. It was strange, they both knew, to be on what amounted to opposite sides. But they were.

"Michael, I just want to warn you to be very careful what you write about this evening. I am not at all sure you know what you're talking about or who you're dealing with. My client has nothing to do with Thelma Pitts or Molly Whipple, or whatever you call her."

"Your client Mr. Flannery?"

"That's right. I doubt he even knows who she is."

There was a long silence. The clerk watched them staring at one another, lost interest, and went back to work.

Carolina felt completely calm, not at all the way he imagined he would. No pain, no sense of loss. He looked straight into her eyes, until she broke, and started flipping through the documents he'd handed her.

"Let me get this straight," he said. "You represent Jimmy Flannery, and to your knowledge he has never met a woman named Molly Whipple or Thelma Pitts?"

Marie looked back at him. "To my knowledge, that's correct."

"You're sure?"

"I'm sure."

Carolina sighed without realizing it. "If you learn differently before six o'clock tonight, give me a call."

She looked at him. "I can save you the trouble right now. Mr. Flannery will have no comment."

He checked to make sure he had all his papers. Marie went back to looking at the documents. It was strange, Carolina thought, how they had once been so close. It was only for a little while, he recognized. They had met because his profession intersected with hers, and there had been a mutual attraction. But now the attraction was gone, suffocated by his need to break a story and her obligation to a client.

"See you around, Marie."

She didn't answer.

He walked out of the courthouse. He never saw her hand shake as she laid the documents down.

Thelma Pitts, dressed in a spanking new blue canvas prison uniform, was arraigned before a federal magistrate later that day. A small crowd that included Carolina and Bert Schumacher looked on as she was charged with being a felon in possession of a firearm. An exceptionally short prosecutor with thinning hair and a perennially arrogant expression explained that the United States expected to bring additional charges after convening a grand jury. After a brief hearing, Pitts was ordered detained.

A few minutes later, Pitts was led outside by two U.S. marshals to a waiting van. She tried to clutch her hands against her shoulders, but was prevented by the handcuffs and belly chains. A few reporters tried to shout questions. Carolina said nothing. He couldn't take his eyes off the ragged blisters on the side of her face. The blisters wept in the heat, almost, but not quite, as if Thelma Pitts were crying.

As the van drove off, he turned and almost ran into Schumacher.

"Rule 48-G," Carolina said.

"Return of service on a warrant," Schumacher said. "Lot of reporters don't know about it. You get what you need?"

"I'm okay," Carolina said. "I'll be better tonight."

"Good," the agent said. He turned to leave.

"How you feeling?"

Schumacher stopped. "Better, thanks. Got discharged this morning. I'm supposed to be home sleeping. But I didn't want to miss this."

"What about your partner?"

"Ernie"—the agent shook his head—"it's a crying shame. Someone in D.C. notified him last night that he's getting a special assignment. In Topeka."

Carolina's package led the broadcast at six o'clock. It included a full screen graphic quoting Marie Brine denying that her client Jimmy Flannery had anything to do with Thelma Pitts. The graphic cut to a shot of Flannery walking with Pitts into Adesso's on the East Side.

"There goes her credibility," Shirley said.

"He could have lied to her," Carolina said. "Or told her a half truth."

"Or maybe she just didn't think you could prove a connection. You can't trust lawyers."

"That's not fair," Carolina said. He watched as his package rolled through more graphics, detailing the documents seized from the real estate office, and concluded with a slo-mo shot of Pitts shuffling off to the marshal's van, then a dissolve into the video of the explosion of Mitty's boat.

"Great stuff, Michael. Michael? Hello?"

"What? Oh, thanks."

Shirley leaned back in her chair and lit up another cigarette. "You look like you've got other things on your mind. Why don't you get out of here?"

He walked back to his desk and picked up the phone. The hospital operator put the call through to Carla's room without any questions.

"Michael, I saw it! Great story!"

"How are you feeling?" She sounded much better than when he had seen her the day before.

"The doctor says I can be discharged tomorrow. You going to help nurse me back to full health?" There was a teasing sound to her voice that made him smile.

"If I had to guess," he said, "I'd say you were leering."

"You'd have guessed right. Michael, that piece, it was fantastic. What do you think it will do to the gambling referendum?"

He hadn't thought of it before. It was a story, a good story, but things had happened so quickly that day that he'd never considered its larger significance. Carla's question was unsettling. The images of his father and mother, of those long-ago moments in Iowa, came rattling back. He had kept the memories suppressed, but now they welled up once more. Carolina hated casinos, big ones, little ones, or those that were only in the planning stages.

"Let's hope it's a bust," he said.

D espite the apparent resolution of questions surrounding the death of the so-called "clamcake bomber," Sally Generous made another lame attempt to capitalize on the event on behalf of herself and Save the Chowder. A week and a half after the explosions at the Gaspee Days parade, Generous called a press conference to announce her candidacy for Congress.

Before a small crowd of well-intentioned environmentalists and an even smaller group of skeptical journalists, Generous claimed that Mitty Navel had actually been a tool of various polluters, whose goal was to destroy Generous and her organization. Asked to produce some evidence in support of the allegation, Sally gamely changed the subject to how she favored raising corporate taxes to fund further research into aquaculture and cleaning up the bay.

A few days after the announcement, a group of disgruntled quahoggers requested a copy of Generous's financial statement from the Federal Elections Commission. The quahoggers then mailed the statement–anonymously–to a political columnist at the Providence *Herald*. The next day the *Herald* ran a page-one story detailing Generous's numerous stockholdings in a variety of oil companies, electric and gas utilities, and a nuclear power plant in Paraguay. Reeling from allegations that she had betrayed Save the Chowder, Generous called a new press conference to explain that the stocks were an inheritance from an uncle. What little support existed for Generous's candidacy nevertheless disintegrated, and she quietly withdrew from the race.

The Ocean State Preservation Society announced the results of its analysis of the wooden remains found in Stillhouse Cove the week after Thelma Pitts's arrest. The society's one-page press release confirmed that the pieces belonged not to the long-lost *Gaspee,* but to an old speedboat used to run bootleg liquor into Cranston during Prohibition. The news garnered fifteen-second stories on two local newscasts, and a two-paragraph story in the *Herald.*

The evening was cool and comfortable, and Thayer Street was loaded with students newly arrived or newly returned to Brown or the Rhode Island School of Design. Michael Carolina and Carla Tattaglia made their way through the crowds, past the Thai restaurant and the Tex-Mex place and the army-navy store. The Avon was showing a new film, and a line was forming for the early show.

"It's so nice to be past Labor Day," Carla said. "I've never been so happy to see summer come to an end."

"Couldn't take the heat?" Carolina asked. "I thought you got the breeze down in Edgewood."

"Not this year," she said. "Now where are we going again?"

"We're already here." The restaurant was located in a building that fronted Thayer Street. The dark green sign announced that it was called Kabob 'N Curry.

A host smiled and seated them near the window, and they spent a few minutes watching the passersby. A waiter brought a bottle of white wine and a pair of menus.

"You go ahead and order," Carla said.

Carolina did: chicken tikka masala, shahi paneer, and barra-kabob, with raita and an order of garlic nan bread.

"It smells wonderful in here," Carla said. "All those spices. Now what was that you want to try?"

"Barra-kabob." Carolina smiled. "Possibly the best lamb chops you'll ever taste."

They both sipped some wine. Carla looked better again, Carolina decided. She had almost regained the tan she had lost after the shooting. She wore her hair down around her shoulders and it framed her face perfectly. She noticed him watching her, and she offered a dazzling smile.

"You glad to be back at work?"

"It's okay," she said. "They still won't let me back aboard a boat. I'll probably be driving a car until the spring. To be honest with you, I don't know whether I'm going to stay with DEM."

Carolina raised his eyebrows. The news was a complete surprise.

"What are you going to do?"

"Well." Carla looked at him seriously. "I hear there's an opening at ATF."

"What?"

"Just kidding," she said, laughing. "I know how much you love those guys."

"They're not all bad," Carolina said. "I actually respect Schumacher. And O'Mara's not around anymore."

"The truth is," Carla said, "I was thinking about opening my own business."

"The restaurant?"

"Someday," Carla said. "But with all this great law enforcement training I have, I thought maybe I could open my own investigation business."

"You're kidding."

"No," Carla said. "Not at all. I don't like having bosses any more than you do."

Dinner arrived, and the discussion of career choices got lost in the smell of the spices and the marinated lamb.

"God," Carla said. "This is better than Chinese. Listen, you know I'm now a loyal Channel Three viewer, but I hear one of your competitors released a poll yesterday. Sounds like that gambling referendum is going to go down in flames."

"I heard," Carolina said, tearing off a piece of the garlic nan. The bread was soft and rich, and melted in his mouth.

"Doesn't that make you feel good?"

Carolina shrugged. "The tribes are still looking for a casino, and they'll probably get one. There's still a dog track in Lincoln, and crap games run by the mob in Silver Lake and up on Federal Hill."

"Don't be so cynical." She smiled at him again, and the bad thoughts he held faded a bit. "At least admit that you made a difference," she said, sliding a tanned hand into his. "That counts for something."

"Okay, maybe it does," he said. "But not as much as you."

They sat there for a moment, looking at one another. Then he felt her foot, touching his ankle, and rising slowly up his left leg.

"What do you want to do after dinner?"

"I thought you wanted to see a movie," Carolina said.

"I did," she said. "But now I have something else in mind."

"Sounds like it could be risky."

"No," Carla said. "It's a sure thing."